Once Upon A Kiss

Susan Mendonca

SCHOLASTIC INC.
New York Toronto London Auckland Sydney

For my editor, Ann Reit,
whose idea it was to write a fairy tale.

ISBN 0-590-33267-8

12 11 10 9 8 7 6 5 4 3 2 1   6   5 6 7 8 9/8

Printed in the U.S.A.   06

A Wildfire Book

WILDFIRE® TITLES FROM SCHOLASTIC

I'm Christy by Maud Johnson
Beautiful Girl by Elisabeth Ogilvie
Dreams Can Come True by Jane Claypool Miner
An April Love Story by Caroline B. Cooney
Yours Truly, Love, Janie by Ann Reit
The Best of Friends by Jill Ross Klevin
Second Best by Helen Cavanagh
Take Care of My Girl by Carol Stanley
Secret Love by Barbara Steiner
Nancy & Nick by Caroline B. Cooney
Senior Class by Jane Claypool Miner
Junior Prom by Patricia Aks
He Loves Me Not by Caroline Cooney
Good-bye, Pretty One by Lucille S. Warner
Write Every Day by Janet Quin-Harkin
Christy's Choice by Maud Johnson
The Wrong Boy by Carol Stanley
The Boy for Me by Jane Claypool Miner
Class Ring by Josephine Wunsch
Phone Calls by Ann Reit
Just You and Me by Ann Martin
Homecoming Queen by Winifred Madison
Holly in Love by Caroline B. Cooney
Spring Love by Jennifer Sarasin
No Boys? by McClure Jones
Blind Date by Priscilla Maynard
That Other Girl by Conrad Nowels
Little Lies by Audrey Johnson
Broken Dreams by Susan Mendonca
Love Games by Deborah Aydt
Call Me by Jane Claypool Miner
Miss Perfect by Jill Ross Klevin
On Your Toes by Terry Morris
Christy's Love by Maud Johnson
Nice Girls Don't by Caroline B. Cooney
Christy's Senior Year by Maud Johnson
Kiss and Tell by Helen Cavanagh
The Boy Next Door by Vicky Martin
Angel by Helen Cavanagh
Out of Bounds by Eileen Hehl
Senior Dreams Can Come True by Jane Claypool Miner
Loving that O'Connor Boy by Diane Hoh
Love Signs by M. L. Kennedy
My Summer Love by Elisabeth Ogilvie
Once Upon a Kiss by Susan Mendonca

One

"Oh, Paula, this will be the most exciting party of our senior year!" declared Laurie Wellington, my best friend of the past eleven years.

We were in Laurie's bedroom. I was pinning the waist of her Cinderella costume, which she planned to wear to Beecher High's New Year's Eve Costume Party.

"Well, all I can say is, with your enthusiasm, you ought to find your Prince Charming there."

A misty look came over Laurie's round blue eyes, which were the same satin-blue as the gown. "Those are hard to come by, Paula. But I'm not giving up!" She twirled daintily in front of the oval floor mirror, lifting the shimmering, ankle-length folds of her skirt.

I thought back on how far Laurie had come since the fall, when her boyfriend, Don, had moved away. At first she was heartbroken about his move to California, and wrote him long letters every day. Then, a couple of months after he left, he wrote to let her know that he was seeing someone else. Laurie and I were certain this never would've happened if he hadn't moved, but that wasn't much consolation. Laurie was crushed, and we had to piece her back together.

This sort of coincided with what happened to me at the end of summer: My boyfriend at the time, Ricky Castle, went out with Carla Brent behind my back. It wouldn't have made me much happier if he had gone out with her right in front of me, but the worst was to have people we both knew tell me about it, and to feel the humiliation creep over my face like some kind of disease.

Needless to say, I was devastated, but in addition was the painful fact that Carla was a friend of mine. We weren't best friends like Laurie and I, but we were pretty close. Once, Carla helped me with a composition about how each of us felt about someone very special. She did hers on her mother, and I did mine on Ricky. Carla was the only one who knew that the subject of my comp was Ricky. I confided in her about him — how crazy I was about him, and what his favorite activities and foods were.

I must have made Ricky sound pretty good, yet I still don't think Carla intended to hurt me — even though she did. Ever since then, she hadn't been able to look me straight in

2

the eye, even when Ricky went away to college and she was still going to Beecher, and kept dating him. My mom said Carla felt guilty, and seeing me made her feel terrible about herself, and that in some way she was in a worse position than I was. I wasn't sure that anyone could feel worse than I did.

Anyway, after that heartbreak, and Don's leaving, Laurie and I formed an unofficial Lonely Hearts Club — just the two of us. We held each other up through the rough times, making sure we pampered ourselves and that we didn't allow ourselves to feel too dejected. Neither of us dated much since then, mainly because we were particular. We looked at different boys, envisioning them for each other, laughing about the possibilities. But I noticed Laurie growing wistful of late. I think she really wanted someone, someone warm, funny, and sweet — like Don.

Personally, I avoided the whole idea of getting involved with another boy. Instead, I plunged headlong into my piano playing, with the intent of someday becoming a concert pianist. At least, I figured that wouldn't disillusion me as Ricky had. Still, sometimes I remembered the good times with Ricky — how it was before he became discontented — and I yearned for that feeling again.

I perched the curled, powdered white wig on Laurie's head, and stuffed her long red-gold hair inside it.

"How do I look?" she asked.

"You're beautiful!" I whispered, standing back to admire our handiwork. Laurie and I had the same body proportions, and were the same height, so we could exchange everything. She wore a half-size larger shoe than I, but other than that, our clothes were interchangeable.

The costumes were provided by Laurie's mom, who was the director of the local college's drama department, and had access to the complete costume wardrobe. Not surprisingly, Laurie was a budding actress herself.

"Pretty stunning, huh?" Laurie allowed herself one more quick spin in front of the mirror. Then she tossed me the silky white dress. "Come on. Let's get to work on Snow White. A prince woke her up with a magic kiss, you know." She winked at me.

"I don't plan on falling asleep, Laurie," I giggled, slipping the cool white fabric over my head. As she zipped me into the dress, I criticized my reflection. "I look washed out," I grumbled.

"Only because it's winter. Wear lots of makeup," Laurie advised.

It was a beautiful dress, but too bad the New Year's party had to be held in midwinter. My skin was very white, and my dark, near-black, shoulder-length hair made me look even paler.

Laurie draped my hair over one shoulder. "Your green eyes are a real plus with that fabulous hair," she said. My hair *was* one of my best features. "Here, try a little blush and lipstick."

I applied both. "There, much better." My friend studied me with approval.

"Are you sure I shouldn't go as Red Riding Hood? Or the wolf?" I sighed. Laurie laughed.

This conversation took place a week before the party. What neither Laurie nor I counted on was her coming down with the flu the day of the gala event.

"You can't be sick!" I wailed to her over the phone.

"I'd have to go on a stretcher like someone from a Poe story, and infect everyone. This is not a fun flu. But I've been thinking . . ." She sneezed. "Since you like the Cinderella costume better than the Snow White one, why don't you go as Cinderella?"

"Wow, really? I was all psyched up for Snow White." I considered for a minute and realized that I did prefer the Cinderella outfit. "I can slip into another skin easy enough. Yes, I'd love to be Cinderella."

"Great! Come over and get the costume, Paula. I'm not getting up, though, if you don't mind. It'll be ready for you . . . even down to the glass slippers." Another lengthy sneeze. "Boy, wait till Ricky sees you in that dress!"

"Ricky?" My heart screeched to a halt when she said his name.

"Uh-oh . . . I wasn't going to mention it,

but I overheard Carla saying she's bringing him to the party."

"Oh, no!" I didn't want to see either Carla or Ricky, especially not at a party.

"You can avoid him, Paula," Laurie said.

"I don't want to spend the whole evening sitting in a corner," I said, already feeling tight and unhappy about skulking around Ricky and Carla all evening.

"You won't have to," Laurie said. "Remember, you'll be wearing a mask all evening. No one will know who you are, much less know that you're uncomfortable. Also, you can flirt with anyone you want, to your heart's content."

I laughed, hanging up, calmed by the realization that I'd be able to hide behind a mask. But would seeing Ricky and Carla together remind me of Ricky and me? And would it also call up the humiliation I'd suffered a few months before?

I decided not to allow those things to happen. I planned to have a great time at the party, in spite of Ricky.

Yet little did I know then how Laurie's flu, and my being Cinderella, was going to change the course of my life.

6

*T*wo

I gathered up the Cinderella costume while
Laurie slept in a fever. I felt bad for her and
for me — the Lonely Hearts wouldn't be together tonight for this event.

Laurie and I had been friends since first
grade. I was the new kid in school, and we
were playing on the monkey bars at recess
when she slipped and fell, knocking a front
tooth loose and cutting her lip. She cried so
hard she couldn't move, and I had to coax her
down from the bars, which wasn't easy. By
the time we got to the nurse's office, we were
both speckled with her blood. While the
nurse examined her, Laurie held my hand
and asked me, "You'll be my friend, won't
you?"

We've been friends ever since, teasing each
other about being "blood" sisters.

When I arrived home with the costume,
my ten-year-old sister, Meg, eyed the dress
with mixed emotions.

7

"That's not white," she noted. "Snow White wears *white*, Paula."

'I realize that, but guess what?" I filled her in on the switcheroo.

"I should've known. Those aren't glass slippers, either." Meg's dark brown eyes took in every detail of the costume lying on my patchwork quilt.

"Yeah, but glass slippers are hard to find, and also breakable, so we have to settle for silver satin pumps. Aren't they pretty?" I slipped one on to show her. It was loose.

"Uh-huh. Can I help you get ready?"

"Sure." During the past year, Meg's interest in clothes had blossomed. Her favorite colors were purple and pink, and she came up with some really ghastly combinations, but she seemed happy with herself.

I heard Mom come in from shopping just as I got out of the shower.

"Hi," she called to whomever was around to hear. Meg ran out to meet her, and I followed, curious to see what she bought.

My older sister, Regina, was with Mom.

"Hi, Reggie. What did you buy?" I asked, sticking my nose into a Macy's bag.

"Nosey." She slapped my hand playfully. "Just a pair of leg warmers and gloves to replace the ones I lost at the game Friday night," she explained, scooting fingers through her short, sleek, dark hair before flouncing onto an oak dining chair. "God, I'm exhausted. Following Mom around the mall is a regular workout."

"Yeah, I know. You need your jogging shoes," I agreed.

"Oh, you girls just have lead feet, that's all. If you grew up in a big city as I did, you'd learn how to bustle around in no time." Our mother knows the fine art of bustling all right, which she doesn't confine to shopping. She is short, thin, and business-like. Her cap of fine blonde hair frames a round, pleasant face, with dark blue eyes and a button nose. This year, she was going back to school to get her B. A., which she tackled like everything else in her life — efficiently.

My sister, Reggie, probably takes after Mom more than Meg and I. She's the athletic type, built solidly, all muscle — but of course, that's because she works out at swimming, jogging, or gymnastics every day. I decided a long time ago that my talents lie in another direction, so I was not one of those little sisters to follow in big sister's footsteps.

When we were little, Reggie and I fought like cats and dogs. It's only in recent years that we've come to adore one another, but don't tell her I said that. I'm not sure that she's quite arrived at the point of adoring *me*, yet. It may be wishful thinking on my part.

"Come and see what I'm wearing tonight." Everyone crowded into my bedroom, which is by no means, big. In fact, it's so tiny there's no way I could ever share my room with either of my sisters, if we had company — which was one of the reasons I picked it when we moved in.

I've hung posters of famous musicians on the eggshell-white walls, and made multi-colored throw pillows for my quilt. I collect china teddy bears which fill up the top of my dresser, along with photos of myself with the orchestra and at piano recitals. My bookshelves are cluttered with paperbacks and sheet music, and of course, my stereo and albums, all organized by music style: classical, blues, pop, etc.

We all huddled around my bed, where my costume still lay in all its splendor.

"Hey, it's great, but weren't you going to be Snow White?" Reggie asked in confusion.

I began to explain, and explained again when my father got home and wanted a replay of the day's events.

My father, Wallace Rizzoni, is the parent I take after. He's always had a great appreciation of music, although he never played an instrument, and took me to orchestra concerts when I was little. He insists that I was the only one who would sit quietly and listen.

He is a short man, with dark curly hair, green eyes like mine, a beard and mustache, and a waistline that lately stretches the buttons on his shirts. He is developing a preference for pullover sweaters that hide his paunch, while my mother insists on limiting his starch intake.

We ate dinner hurriedly that evening. Re-

gina and her boyfriend, Louie, were also
going to a party, on the college campus. Since
Louie's car wasn't running, I would drive
them to their party first. They could get a
ride home with somebody else.

Reggie helped me with the makeup and
the wig, fixing it so none of my dark hair
spilled out. Last of all was the black mask
that we were all required to wear until the
clock struck twelve. Then we all had to un-
mask and kiss our dates, or whoever was
handy.

"You can't tell who you are!" Meg squealed
with delight. "Except you do look like Cinderella."

The dress looked and felt wonderful. It
nipped in at the waist, and flared delicately
into a blue satin bell. The effect was stunning.

I closed my eyes and imagined myself
dancing with Ricky — back when we were
seen everywhere together. I tried to imagine
his reaction to me in this dress, if he knew
it was me. . . .

But he wouldn't know. I planned to keep
my identity a secret — from everyone.

It was a cold night, and since the heater
in the car was on the blink, we had to use
my father's pickup truck, which he used in
his contracting business.

I climbed into the truck seat, gathering
my skirts in behind me, still blinking from
the onslaught of Dad's flashbulbs. He gets

out the camera for every occasion, which he catalogs in slides.

"Boy, are you a knockout, Paula!" Louie exclaimed when he saw me. "Maybe we should do something like that next Halloween, Reggie."

Reggie nudged him in the ribs. "You want to be Cinderella, Louis?" she teased.

"Oh, stop, will you. Me, Prince Charming, and you, Cinderella — or some equally romantic combination," Louie sighed. With his big hook nose, chronic cowlick, and angular face, he didn't look like a Prince Charming. Still he was a very likeable guy. In fact, his personality was so engaging that you forgot he wasn't handsome. Regina thought he was wonderful.

I dropped them off and went on to Beecher's gymnasium, where the party was to be held. A Lionel Richie song wafted out over the frozen night air. I imagined each note chilling in place, glistening like an icicle, forming a perfect score across the black sky. I really wished Laurie was with me.

Clutching my blanket shawl close, I hurried into the warmth.

The gym was decorated with swaths of black crepe paper, on which were pasted cutouts of historical and movie characters, such as Scaramouche and Clark Gable. Other big cutouts hung suspended by threads from the rafters, twirling and catching the softly colored lights.

Colette Stuart, dressed as a witch, singled me out. She was a pretty good friend, so I disguised my voice so that she wouldn't recognize me.

"I'm Sarah Duncan." I did a pretty good imitation of Sarah's high-pitched voice. Colette's giggle let me know that I had really pulled it off! She thought I was Sarah!

"Oh, I think there's a Prince Charming around here somewhere," she said, then steered me through the crowd, consisting of George Washington, Marilyn Monroe, a football player, a wasp, and Kermit the Frog.

"Everybody's fully disguised, aren't they?" I said, checking out the array of costumes.

"They went all out this year. This is going to be the most successful party of the whole year!" Colette handed me a cup of punch, a hot fruity combination.

"This is good."

"Thanks. I made it, by accident. I threw peaches in instead of fruit salad, but it turned out good anyway, I think."

Colette is one of those go-getter, join-everything types. She's president of the Girl's Athletic Association, class treasurer, and active in several clubs. Though we're good friends, we hardly spend time together because of all her involvements.

The lights dimmed, and Colette spun away with George Washington. I sat down — sitting down was no easy feat in this dress — letting my skirts drape over the adjoining seats.

I glanced around the room, looking for Ricky and Carla. My goal was to stay away from them, so I wanted to know exactly where they were. They weren't here yet. I sipped my punch nervously, again wishing Laurie had been able to come.

A Michael Jackson song began. Kermit the Frog asked me to dance.

"Gee, you're beautiful, Cinderella," a familiar voice crowed from within the frog suit. I nearly laughed aloud, recognizing who Kermit was: Eddie Lucci, a short, towheaded tenth-grader who was on the newspaper staff.

I made my voice go an octave higher. "Thank you, Kermit. You're pretty cute, yourself," I twittered.

He laughed. It was difficult to dance fast in my costume. I would be better off waltzing, which few boys knew how to do. Laurie and I took a ballroom dance class once, and loved it. Only trouble was, we didn't have many people to dance with.

The next dance was slow, and the football player, Bill Knowland, asked me.

"You're the most gorgeous thing here," he said appreciatively.

"Why, thank you," I said sweetly. I was beginning to relax.

Sylvia Muhly and Jack Slater cleared the floor with their acrobatic dancing. The couple didn't need to wear masks, as everyone was very aware of their fantastic dance skills. They were going to be on *Dance*

Nights in the spring. We all stood in a circle and clapped as they dipped and twirled to the rocking beat. Jack picked up Sylvia and spun her around, then swept her up in a close embrace. When they finally bowed at the end, the crowd cheered and moved in to hug them both.

Cathy Cummins, as Miss Piggy, told me, "Bill Knowland is just dying to know who you are."

"He'll just have to wait until midnight," I said mysteriously.

I glanced over at Bill, and next to him, stood Ricky, dressed in an early aviator costume. He was probably Wilbur Wright.

I should've known Bill would be near Ricky; they were close friends. And standing right next to Ricky, with her arm linked through his, was Carla.

She was dressed in jodhpurs and a riding jacket, looking slim and pretty. Her dark blonde hair was caught in a pink ribbon and flowed down her back.

Ricky was tall, broad-shouldered, blond, with a self-assured grin that immediately caught one's attention. He was last year's star quarterback at Beecher. Girls went crazy over him, just as they now went crazy over Bill, who had taken his place on the team this year.

How jealous I used to be when girls hung around him after the games. People used to say Ricky and I looked good together, but now they probably said that about he and

Carla. I watched him take Carla's hand and lead her out to the dance floor. The couple swayed so easily to the music, it made me wonder if Ricky had ever really loved me at all.

Carla's face shone. I hoped the same thing didn't happen to her. I hoped he didn't hurt her like he hurt me. Maybe she would be smart enough not to invest all her love in him, as I did.

Oh, well, I told myself, turning away from the dance floor, *life's a lot less troublesome without Ricky, that's for sure.*

Suddenly upset, I grabbed my shawl and strolled outside for a breath of fresh air. I stood out on the deck that overlooked the twinkling lights of the town, nestled in the folds of hills. A few lights peeped from farmhouses across the black landscape like tiny diamonds on velvet.

My heart pounded so loudly in my ears that I didn't hear footsteps approaching, only a twig snapping. I spun around to face a smiling Prince Charming.

Caught completely off-guard, I gripped the wrought-iron railing of the deck. Did I know him? He was tall, chestnut-haired, handsome, of course. Since his eyes were hidden by the mask, I took a quick survey of firm lips, strong wings of cheekbone, a broad nose, hair waving gentle over his ears. His outfit consisted of a cape and ruffled shirt with black slacks.

A low, throaty chuckle rose from deep

inside him, tripping a tremor all the way to my toes.

"Fancy meeting you here," he grinned. "Am I supposed to say, 'Where have you been all my life?'"

"I don't know. Is that one of your lines?" I replied shakily. A prickly, warm flush overtook me.

"You are beautiful, you know." He shook his head. Thin strands of light picked up the reddish tones in his hair. "Now I know exactly how Prince Charming felt. Up until this moment, I haven't really gotten into the part."

I laughed, the tension over Ricky and Carla slowly beginning to dissolve. "Same here."

"I don't have the slightest idea who you are, either," he said, leaning casually against the railing. His cape draped nicely over well-shaped shoulders, and he gestured with his hands while he talked. "But of course, that's part of the intrigue. You might be from out of town."

"Might be." I considered this with amusement. "But you could be, too. You could even be an undercover reporter, gathering a story for a faraway city newspaper."

The prince laughed. "What an imagination. Tell me, do you have any wicked stepsisters?"

"Only two real ones. But they can get pretty wicked at times."

"They don't make you scrub floors, do

they?" Dimples deepened around his mouth.

"No, but our mother does."

He chuckled. "What do you do in your spare time?"

"Play the piano," I replied nonchalantly.

"I should've known. Those are a pianist's fingers." Gently, he lifted my hand. My nails were short half moons, frosted with pink polish for tonight's party. "I bet you're good."

"I'm okay." I shrugged, not wanting to appear immodest. "I'm told I have a good ear."

The prince leaned over and tugged on one of my earlobes. I hoped none of my dark hair was visible from beneath my wig. "Two good ears, it looks like to me. Piano ears."

It was my turn to laugh.

"I'm involved in music, too. I'd like to hear you play sometime," he said, grinning.

"Sure," I answered, without thinking that chances are we'd never see each other. I was feeling as though I existed in a bubble, with Prince Charming and nobody else. One of my favorite songs came on in the gym, and I started to hum dreamily.

"Would you like to dance?" he asked, lifting my hand, which felt suddenly weightless in his.

"Yes, I would."

Out on the floor, his arms closed around my waist, sending arrows of warmth through me. He turned out to be a great dancer, as a prince should be. I told him so.

"You're a good dancer, too," he said, smiling down at me. "But Prince Charming and Cinderella are supposed to be a dazzling spectacle on the dance floor, anyway."

"Definitely."

I closed my eyes and concentrated on the circles of warmth emanating from the spot on my back where his hand pressed, guiding me across the floor. I drifted, loving every minute, every sensation, wanting him to hold me like this forever — until the music ended.

I felt abruptly yanked back to earth. But only for a brief instant.

"Thank you." Prince Charming bowed, then leaned over and brushed his lips across the back of my hand, sending a troop of goose pimples racing along my flesh.

"You're welcome," I replied breathlessly. I realized that I hadn't really been thinking since I laid eyes on this boy. And who was he? There were many good looking boys at Beecher, but I didn't know all of them personally.

But something was happening to me. Carla and Ricky seemed like figures on a distant shore of my mind, and I heard myself talking to Prince Charming about my music and interests, strangely comfortable with him — even though we'd only just met.

Suddenly, from within the gym came the blare of New Year's horns, whistles, and shouts. The prince's arms wove tightly around me. He traced the outline of my lips with his forefinger before his mouth covered mine.

His kiss flared in me, sweet and wild. In response, I linked my arms around his neck, and we remained for a long moment wrapped around each other.

"Masks off!" someone shouted.

"Hey, you two! Masks off!" came the persistent cry.

Grinning, the prince pulled off his mask, revealing coffee-brown eyes, and the rest of his handsome face.

I froze. He was popular, talented Kevin Stevens, from my orchestra period! Fear shot through me, making me tremble uncontrollably. He was one of those guys that girls flocked around — sort of a musical celebrity.

"C'mon, Cinderella, take off your mask," Kevin urged. "What's wrong? Are you bashful?" Playfully, he tugged on the elastic at the side of my mask, but I moved his hand away, my good feelings gone.

Then I ran — through the crowded gym, past a blur of now-famil··· faces. Colette grabbed my arm. "Hey, Sarah, where're you going? The party's not over!" she cried.

"Sorry, I have to go," I mumbled, draping my dragging shawl around my shoulders.

I tripped on the way out, going up some steps, and my shoe fell off. By the time I realized it was missing, there wasn't time to go back and get it. Anyway, after that exit, I couldn't go back inside.

I hopped down to the parking lot, glancing up at the gym as I left. A tall figure wandered around in front of the lighted entrance. The way he walked reminded me of Kevin.

It was a good thing I managed to leave without him catching up with me, I thought, sliding onto the cold upholstery. Sketchy information on Kevin began filtering into my brain: He played in a teen club on weekends, he was chosen as a flute soloist for our upcoming orchestra concert, he was a member of the Honor Society, and didn't he go out with popular Cheryl Wittmer last year?

As the warmth seeped into the truck and defrosted my limbs, I calmed down. The glittering lights of the party became pinpricks in my rearview mirror, then quickly vanished. My evening of being Cinderella dropped back into Fantasyland — where it belonged.

I had gone to the party with no expectations, and yet something had happened. Prince Charming's kisses wiped away the pain of seeing Ricky and Carla together — making me forget, but also making me remember, with their lingering sweetness.

Three

When I got home from the party, I slipped off my one shoe and crouched in front of the fireplace to catch the last warmth from the dying embers. The house was quiet. Everyone was asleep, thankfully, so I didn't have to explain why I only wore one shoe home, and why I was torn between wanting to cry and laugh.

When I was warmed through, I climbed the stairs to my room, slipped out of the Cinderella dress, and welcomed the comfort of my bed.

But I couldn't fall asleep right away. I wondered what Kevin Stevens, alias Prince Charming, was doing at that moment. I wondered if he was looking for me, or whether he'd gone back inside and found a more willing Cinderella. With my fingertip, I outlined my lips, remembering once more how his lips felt on mine.

I thought of Ricky and I together, as we were before we broke up.

I was at a football game. Laurie and I were huddled together in the bleachers, with my father's plaid picnic blanket draped over our knees. Ricky had just made a touchdown. The crowd went wild, nearly drowning us with its commotion. I could see Ricky, leaping up and down, brandishing the football in the air.

Afterwards, like always, the cheerleaders and pompon girls surrounded the players, hugging and congratulating them. When Ricky whipped off his helmet, I saw his jubilant face: a streak of mud across his ruddy cheek, his hair tousled, his eyes gleaming. . . .

I wanted to be with him, to place a congratulatory kiss on his cheek, to stand in that electric circle of excitement. With difficulty, I pressed towards him through the crowd of students and faculty. And just when I was a few yards away, Ricky turned while talking with teammates, and walked away from me.

Of course, it was coincidental. But it scared me, because little things like this kept happening between Ricky and I. Things kept coming between us: practices — both mine and his — cancelled dates for one reason or another. Finally, he told me he needed to spend more time with his friends.

I went to meet him by the boys' gym a half hour later, as planned. Just as I turned the corner of the locker room building, I wished I could stop my feet from plodding in that direction, toward the floodlit entrance where the glow turned the pavement bright yellow.

In that buttery triangle of light stood Ricky and Carla. She touched the tip of his nose with her pinky, and leaned forward.

I coughed, not meaning to. She stopped what she was doing and turned. Her mouth dropped open when she saw me.

Not my friend, Carla!

The idea was too unbelievable. "Hi, Ricky! Hi, Carla," I greeted them, my voice brittle against the cold night air.

Ricky's face went through a series of changes when he looked at me, but his lips were ready with a brief kiss.

Carla said hi, stiffly. We talked about the outcome of the game. My fear evaporated when she said she was just congratulating Ricky on his playing. I smiled. Ricky threaded his arm through mine and we went to the after-game dance.

Ricky was tall, and my head only reached his lips, so I had to stand on tiptoe to kiss him. We fit together very well for dancing, though. I could snuggle up against his broad chest, and listen to his heartbeat as we glided around the room. I liked having his heartbeat and the music in sync, and our rhythm following both.

I was in another world when I was in his arms. I felt so close to him. He was mine then, and I never dreamed of it ending.

So I wasn't ready, and I didn't expect it when it came — when he told me he was dating Carla.

And then I thought about how Ricky and I got together. I knew who he was, but that was all. I was sitting cross-legged on the carpet in the school library, reading. He tripped over me.

"Oh, sorry," he grinned down at me. "You're Paula, right?"

"Yes." I gazed up at him, once he recovered himself. In one glance, I took in his long legs, football shoulders, and engaging blue eyes.

"Well, Paula, has anyone ever tripped over you before?" He winked.

The sunlight poured in from a nearby window, slanting across his face and making his hair glisten. A piece of me was floating, like a dust mote, as if it wanted to be caught up and carried away.

"No," I said. "Most people look where they're going."

He laughed, earning a disapproving glance from Mrs. Petrie, the librarian.

"Okay, you got me that time." He flopped down beside me, then dug in his pocket for something. "Can you help me find this book, by any chance?"

I flipped a lock of my hair over my shoulder to take a closer look at what was written on the slip of paper in his hand: *The Life and Times of Joe Namath.*

"You have to look in the card catalog. Or the biography section, under the author's name," I said.

Ricky struck a helpless pose, so I assisted him. It turned out he had a book report due in two days, so that night he came over and we worked on it together.

The next time I saw him, a Monday morning, he kissed me.

"That's for helping me get an A," he said. When he sauntered down the hall to his next class, I knew I was hopelessly in love with him.

We were together for six months, which seemed so brief to me. One day Laurie and I walked into The Soda Shop, a favorite after-school hangout, and that's when I heard about Ricky and Carla.

Betty Lyn Mays came over to me and asked, "Oh, I guess you're not going out with Ricky anymore, Paula?"

I mumbled something unintelligible, out of shock, and then: "Well, he's been seen around with Carla Brent. Didn't you know? Aren't you and Carla friends?"

It was a backhanded, sloppy way to find out your boyfriend isn't true to you. I felt like I'd been hit from behind. As the reality worked on me, I gradually pulled together all the pieces of a puzzle I didn't want to figure out — remembering Ricky and Carla after the game, the broken dates, the excuses. . . .

It was summer when Ricky and I split up. We stood in my backyard on a day where the heat hung in the air, shimmering, and even the flowers looked rumpled and wilting.

I wondered why I absorbed those common details while my personal life was ready to fall apart — and there was nothing I could do to stop it.

"I'm going out with Carla now," Ricky said.

"That's all you're going to tell me?" I was on the verge of tears, but I wouldn't cry in front of him.

He shrugged. "I wanted to keep seeing you, too, Paula. You know how I feel about you. . . ."

"I do now. And please, don't try to explain anything, Ricky. Just go, please!"

I simply wanted him to leave, right away. I wanted no explanation, and I didn't want to have to look at him for another minute. My pain was like a giant envelope with me inside it, already sealed.

" 'Bye." Ricky couldn't meet my gaze, which was probably fierce enough to singe his eyebrows off.

After he was gone, I surveyed the garden: the tire swing he and I used to swing on together, the kickball we played with in the field, Meg's tree house where Ricky kissed me the second time, or maybe it was the third. . . .

Then my eye followed the neatly spaced

prints Ricky left in the grass. I plucked a few blades of grass, went inside, and stuck them in my diary.

I wrapped myself around my pillow. My heart moved over the bittersweet scenes, looking for clues, while my mind tried to convince me there were none.

I slid out of bed, and found my diary in a desk drawer. It had been months since I made an entry in it, but I found the blades of grass, dried and pressed between two pages.

I believe I put them there to remind myself what it was like to fall in love, and what it was like to have a broken heart — just in case I might forget.

For a long time I lay in bed, thinking that even though I might sometimes yearn for what Ricky and I used to share, I didn't honestly know if it was worth being crushed later on.

F*our*

"I left the party before anyone could discover who I was, after finding out I'd kissed Kevin Stevens," I explained to Laurie, who sat up in her bed, wide-eyed with amazement. I held up the blue gown, smoothing the creases out of it before hanging it in her closet.

Laurie giggled. "You must've been nervous about seeing Carla and Ricky there, even though they didn't know who you were," she deduced. The color had come back into her complexion, and she looked much better.

"I guess nothing short of a suit of armor would make me feel comfortable around them," I admitted.

"Guess not." Laurie paged through the *Seventeen* magazine that lay across her lap. "Sounds like you had fun, in spite of them."

"Hmmm." I picked up the single satin shoe. "By the way, I lost the other shoe. It fell off as I was leaving. . . ."

The dawning look of horror on Laurie's face made me laugh. I clapped my hands against my cheeks as I realized the significance. "Oh, no. Did I really do that?"

"Paula, this is almost too much to believe. It is sounding suspiciously like a Cinderella story." She shook her head. "First, you kiss Prince Charming on New Year's Eve, while upset about Ricky. And — don't tell me — you didn't go back for the shoe when you discovered it missing, because you were afraid you'd run into Kevin, right?"

"Right."

"I never should've lent you the shoes. They're too big for you. Now, if I remember the fairy tale correctly, Prince Charming finds the glass slipper and searches the entire kingdom for the girl who fits it."

"Yes, but this is real life, and a lot of people wear a size seven and a half," I reminded her. "And besides, everything between Kevin and me was purely platonic. This should've happened to you, Laurie. It's your costume and your shoes. I'm the wrong Cinderella, I wear the wrong size shoe. Everything about this is wrong, wrong, wrong!"

"Don't say that, Paula. Something right will come out of it." Laurie patted my hand soothingly, suppressing a giggle.

I nodded. "I'm really sorry about the shoe. I'll buy the theater department a new pair."

"Never mind. The other one will turn up, I'm sure." Laurie lay back against a stack of pillows, lifting her reddish-gold mane off the back of her neck. "I can't believe it. I just can't believe it," she whispered, and then we both burst out laughing.

By Monday morning, Laurie was completely recovered. She drove us both to school. When we arrived, everyone was talking about Saturday's party, so I filled her in on who was dressed as who and what.

Beecher High was particularly bustling that Monday morning, because students were returning from a week's holiday vacation, as well as bubbling with post-party excitement.

"Boy, did I miss out," Laurie grumbled, twisting a stray hair behind her ear as she twirled the combination lock of our shared locker.

I took out the books we would both need for morning classes. "I know. The Lonely Hearts are better off in pairs," I sighed. "You wouldn't believe how I missed you when I had to walk into the gym all by myself."

Just then, Kevin Stevens strolled past with Kate Greenley, a vivacious, auburn-haired cheerleader. He didn't notice us because he was talking and laughing with her. Laurie chattered about her geography assignment, while I half eavesdropped on Kevin's conversation.

They were talking about the party. Kate complimented Kevin on his costume. Kevin couldn't remember what Kate was dressed as, and she reminded him: Dorothy from the Wizard of Oz.

Laurie and I walked to her first class. "Oh, Kevin and his friend Stanley Kolby are in this class." She winked at me. "Just for the record."

"Lucky you," I muttered under my breath. "See you at lunch."

The next three classes were largely spent recapping what we did on our Christmas vacation, and topped with homework assignments guaranteed to get us back into the swing of things.

Laurie and I met at the snack bar at the beginning of the noon hour. "People are curious about Cinderella," she told me as we trooped into the lunchroom. "I overheard Beebee Casey and Kate Greenley talking about the dress, and how good you looked."

"Really?" I sighed. "Too bad I have to remain anonymous. I can't even bask in the praise."

Laurie clucked her tongue. "The girls asked Kevin if he knew who Cinderella was, and he had to tell them he had no idea. Colette said she thought Cinderella was Sarah Duncan, but later she found out Sarah was dressed as Queen Elizabeth, so Kevin's thoroughly confused. He wants to find out who she is."

"But he never will," I said firmly, taking a large bite of my roast beef sandwich.

My next class was orchestra — which I shared with Kevin.

Kevin played clarinet and flute in orchestra, but I heard he played other instruments in his band. For the past month, we had been working on a medley from *Star Wars*, and a mixture of popular tunes, plus some Gershwin, all in preparation for *Blend of Old and New*, our next school concert.

The flute section was behind me as I sat at the piano, so it wasn't easy to see Kevin . . . if I wanted to, that is. I did notice he was wearing a blue sweater with white reindeers marching across the chest, and his hair was freshly combed.

He played a new flute solo — one never played in class before. Goose bumps rose on my arms, while listening to it, and when Kevin finished playing, I left my seat to speak to him.

"That was beautiful," I told him. "Where did you hear that wonderful song?"

"I wrote it," Kevin smiled, his whole face lighting up. He placed his flute back in its blue velvet-lined case.

"Really?" I was awed. A composer. I walked back to the piano to gather up my music.

A moment later, Kevin stood in the place where Mr. McEllis stood when he conducted. "Just a minute, everybody!" Kevin called. Everyone turned to listen.

"Would the girls please stay after for a

few minutes? I have to try out an experiment." From a brown leather briefcase, which I gathered he carried his music in, he produced a shoe—*the Cinderella shoe*.

I stifled a gasp.

"I'm looking for Cinderella," he explained earnestly, but a snicker traveled throughout the group. A few boys had stayed to see what Kevin was up to.

"We all are, Stevens," one boy yelled from the threshold.

"It's a futile search," another boy added, scooting out the door.

"Not in this case, it isn't," Kevin said with determination. "I would like to try this shoe on every girl in this class before she leaves. It should only take five minutes."

"Oh, for God's sake, I'll be late for my next class," Kate Greenley exclaimed. "Can't you do this tomorrow?"

Kevin started toward her. "Well, I can do you right now, if you like."

I tried to think of a way out, without bringing attention to myself. Of course, I could say I would be late for my next class, too, but then he might be more suspicious of me. I saw the way he scrutinized Kate before he tried to slip the shoe on her foot. It didn't fit.

"Ouch, well, don't try and force it on," she grumbled. "If the shoe doesn't fit. . . ."

"Thanks for being a good sport, Kate." He grinned at her, the hint of laughter behind those coffee-brown eyes.

Kate fled the classroom, scooping music into her backpack as she went.

"How about you, Beebee?" Kevin asked sweetly.

Beebee sighed, and flopped down on one of the metal chairs. She was petite, and I knew she wouldn't wear a seven and a half, even if she had clown feet. "It swims on me," she replied, handing back the shoe. "Even with wool socks."

Alana Collins came over next, and was more than willing to try on the shoe. She made eyes at Kevin, and I thought, Oh, here we go. But the shoe didn't fit, it was too big for her, too. "Darn," she exclaimed. "I would just love to be Cinderella."

"Too bad. Better luck next time." Kevin smiled at her.

Jeannie Winters sat down in front of him, slid her foot daintily out of her ankle boot, and smiled. "I know I'm not the one, because I was dressed as Charlotte the Spider," she said, tossing her long, coal-black hair over a shoulder. The shoe was too small, by about half a size.

"Thanks, Jeannie," Kevin said.

"Let me know who the lucky winner is," she commented, as she sailed out of the music room.

"I'll have the news posted in the main hallway," Kevin called after her, then he turned to regard me with amusement.

My toes were curled up in my shoes, dreading exposure to Kevin's test. I was wearing my duck shoes, not exactly your most fashionable footwear, but nice and practical for tromping around in bad weather.

"Well, Paula? How about it?" Kevin held the shoe out to me in the palm of his hand. He seemed to be reading my face. I hoped he couldn't tell that I was remembering how he kissed me, as I kicked off one duck shoe. I felt his hand slide over the bottom of my foot, almost as if he were tickling me.

Looking down at the silver high heel brought back a flood of recent memories, so sharp and stunning that I suddenly felt dizzy. I took a moment to clear my head before meeting Kevin's soft brown gaze again.

"It's . . . uh, a little loose," I stumbled, hoping he didn't notice me do that. I was just hoping I wasn't a dead giveaway. Why did he have to be so cute? And why was I so affected?

We were the only two people left in the music room, so our voices echoed.

"Yeah, it is. Kevin ran his thumb sort of absently over my toes. A thrill ran down my back.

Then the last bell rang, and I realized I was late for class. I yanked off the shoe and handed it to him. "I'm late for class," I said, pulling my bag along behind me.

"I'm sorry," Kevin said. "Tell your next teacher it was all my fault.

I couldn't help myself. I smiled. "I will."

Well, the rest of the afternoon I was a

wreck. I hoped lots of girls at my high school wore a size seven and a half shoe. I hope poor Kevin got thoroughly confused, because he shouldn't go snooping around, trying to find Cinderella like that. Everybody was going to think he was slightly mad.

By the end of the afternoon, I was pretty much able to forget (or shove to the back of my mind) the way he looked at me when the shoe didn't fit, and my toes had finally stopped curling in my duck shoes. There was a puzzled look in his eyes. I hoped it wasn't because he had figured out that the reason I lost the shoe in the first place, was because it was too big!

Did Kevin find me attractive in "real life"? I wondered. I hastily brushed the questions out of my mind. There wasn't going to be a chance to find out. I refused to let him find out who the real Cinderella was.

After school, Laurie and I met at our locker. "You won't believe what Kevin Stevens did today in my last period class."

I gasped. "What?" I had an idea what Laurie would say.

"He made everyone try on that blasted shoe, and d'ya know what?" Laurie sighed, and cranked the dial of our combination lock. "Honestly, I can't believe this is real. I have to keep slapping my face to find out if this is some sort of sick dream or something. The shoe, of course, fits *me*, Paula. We didn't think of that. We didn't even think that he'd come around with it, trying to find Cinderella. I thought you told me your relationship was purely platonic?"

"Well, uh, I thought so," I stammered.

"I've got news for you, it isn't." Laurie looked at me through tearful china-blue eyes. "He asked me out, Paula. I don't know what to do. I think you should tell him that you're Cinderella."

"I don't want him to know, Laurie," I pleaded with her. We trudged out to the car, and climbed in, rubbing our mittened hands together against the cold. "I want him to think you're Cinderella, if you don't mind. You can't mind going out with him, he's really nice," I said encouragingly.

"Paula." Laurie stepped on the brakes hard, just before we entered the state route. She stared at me in surprise. "You can't just hand over a guy to me like this and say, 'Go out with him.' It's just weird. It's like one of those goofy dating services, where all you're given is this data sheet on the person, and you never can match the face with what's on the sheet."

"This is not like that at all. You're doing me a favor, Laurie," I explained hurriedly. "There is no way it's safe for me to go out with a guy like him. He's too much like Ricky. He's far too popular, and girls chase him all over the place. Just today, he was with some girl," I said, suddenly unable to remember who it was I'd seen him with in the hall.

"So you think I'd have better luck?" Laurie countered, turning to face me as she came to a stoplight. "I'm a member of the Lonely Hearts, too, you know."

"I'm sure you would." I tried to sound convincing, because I *was* sure she'd have better luck with that type than I did. "You're not as much of a marshmallow as I am. And also, if you decide you're not attracted to him, you don't have to keep going out with him. Try it just once, Laurie, for my sake," I pleaded, covering her hand with mine.

She rolled her eyes. We were driving down the rutted road to her house, past the pond, which was still and reflected the gray sky like a looking glass. As she turned into the driveway, she finally gave me an answer.

"Okay, Paula, I'll do it. For *you*. But I'm not happy about this. I think you should be honest. It's you he's after. Don't you think he'll figure out I'm not the right girl?"

"I don't think so. I didn't tell him that much about myself, but he's involved in music, so he'll probably bring that up." We got out of the car and strolled up the pathway to the front door.

Laurie's house is actually a winterized summer cabin. I call it "Abe Lincoln's cabin," because it looks just like those pictures of Abe's first home. The woods meet the backyard, and curve around the front in a giant horseshoe.

"Well, then, anything I need to know about music, I can just ask you," she said, sighing.

The fragrant scent of the wood-burning stove assaulted us as we entered.

"Hi, girls," Mrs. Wellington greeted us. She was polishing the oak dining table when we strolled in. She possessed the same delicate features and hair color as her daughter. "I've got something to show you," she said, leaving her chore to go to the couch, where she picked up a shoe.

One hand rested on her hip, while she dangled the high heel by one finger. "Look what arrived at our drama department today."

Laurie and I exchanged glances. "One of my shoes," Laurie stated flatly.

"One of *our* shoes from our costume room . . . I believe one of a pair Paula borrowed for the party?" She turned to address me.

It was embarrassing, losing the college's shoe. Then I saw the label *Berkshire Community College Drama Dept.* on the insole. "I thought Kevin gave you the shoe, Laurie," I said, perplexed about this whole thing.

"No! He didn't. He kept it. I was so shocked I didn't think about taking it from him," Laurie said, blinking in round-eyed astonishment.

"Which gave him a chance to do additional research." I smlied grimly as Mrs. Wellington went on to explain how she came by the shoe.

"A young man dropped it off to the department this afternoon. He spoke to my assistant Marcy. Apparently, he found it at Beecher's New Year's Eve party. He danced with the young lady who borrowed it."

"And," she grinned while relating this part, "he said he found Cinderella. When he explained, Marcy told him she was pretty sure my daughter did borrow a Cinderella costume last week for a Saturday night party."

I explained my version of the story: meeting Kevin at the party, fleeing and losing the shoe, and today trying on the shoe in class.

"How romantic." Mrs. Wellington put her palms together and beamed. "Are you going out with him, Paula?"

"Well, uh, no, I'm not," I stumbled. "You see, Laurie's going to, because I'm not really interested in him."

Her gaze took in both of us, sitting close together. "Oh, well, Marcy did say he was very cute and very nice."

"He is," I replied simply, thinking of all the complicated reasons why those two qualities weren't enough to convince me to go out with Kevin Stevens. Wild horses couldn't make me go out with him, I decided.

Laurie giggled. "Paula's giving him to me," she said, which made me burst out laughing, too.

Mrs. Wellington looked naturally puzzled. "Sounds odd, but I guess you both know what you're doing."

"It's in our best interests, Mrs. Wellington," I assured her.

Laurie grabbed a bag of chocolate chip

cookies and we went up to her room to do our homework. She took the desk, while I sprawled out on the rag rug.

Her room is painted yellow and she has bright orange pillows arranged on her round futon bed. Posters gleaned from the college drama department, advertising musicals and plays, adorn the walls.

Laurie generally does things in an organized, upright way. I always envied her desktop, for instance. She has a spotless blotter and a little pot of pens which no one ever snitches from . . . and all of them work. Her pencils are always kept sharp. And there is fresh paper in the top drawer, all set to go.

We got ourselves situated, then Laurie turned to me and said, "See? Even my mom thinks it's weird that you're not going to go out with Kevin. And even weirder that I am."

"You are? You are!" I hugged her fiercely. She was now getting the idea. She shook her head, and we got back to work. I was smack in the middle of a geometry problem when the telephone rang.

Laurie pushed back her chair and strode across the room to the phone. She has her own personal line, which means she can talk to absolutely anyone for as long as she wants, without parent or sibling interference.

"Oh, hi," she said casually into the receiver, but I know by the funny wink she gave me that a boy was calling.

"Saturday night? Hmmm, let's see." I loved her let-me-check-my-schedule tone of voice. She pressed her palm over the receiver. "It's Kevin," she whispered. "He's asking me out. What shall we do?"

"Say yes," I urged. I smiled to let her know it was absolutely A-okay with me.

To Kevin, she said, "Yes, I can make it. Okay, see you tomorrow. 'Bye."

"You have a date!" I squealed in excitement. Forgetting, of course, that Saturday nights Laurie and I usually do something together, and this would leave me with nothing to do. But the date would be good for Laurie, I told myself. She needed to date more.

"I guess so," she mumbled, stunned, as if she couldn't quite believe what was happening. "For someone who hasn't even participated in a fairy tale, my life is sure starting to look like one."

"Face it, Laurie, you've been looking for another fairy tale romance. Kevin is definitely not shy, either, like Don was. Remember how that bugged you about him, he was so unsociable? Well, you won't have to worry about that with Kevin."

"I guess not. But I keep thinking, he talks to me as though we're on more familiar terms. Like we've kissed," she said.

"Well, you have, in a way of speaking," I told her.

She looked at me for a moment and grinned. "Then you have to do one thing for me, Paula, before I go out with him."

"What?" She could ask anything of me

now. I'd even crawl on my hands and knees across the Beecher quad for this one.

"Please show me how you kissed Kevin." Her grin split into a flurry of giggles.

I rolled over onto my back and started to laugh.

A pillow sailed through the air and landed on my stomach. "Here, use this pillow to give me a demo on kissing Kevin Stevens," Laurie said.

So I did. I closed my eyes, remembering his fiery touch, and the rippling sensation that filled me when our lips met. Of course, the dry cotton pillow slip left a lot to be desired romantically, but my memories of Kevin were still fresh and sharp.

"Wow!" Laurie exclaimed when I finished my demonstration. "That must've either been some kiss, or you're some actress."

She looked small in her sweatshirt mini dress. I thought about how much she wanted to find somebody to make her forget about Don, someone who was a lot of fun, and I just knew Kevin could be that person . . . even if he did kiss me first.

"Well," I told her conspiratorially. "If you kiss him like that, he'll never know the difference."

The look she gave me said she couldn't quite believe that, but then I continued with my demo, and we both burst out laughing again.

F^{ive}

On Saturday, Laurie and I went shopping for new jeans for her date that evening. Mom had lent me her charge card to use in case I saw something I wanted, with strict orders not to go over fifty dollars. I also had some Christmas money that I was itching to spend.

We went to TJ Max, where we can always find bargains on jeans. It was one of those days where everything I tried on I wanted. Laurie leafed through the racks, getting frustrated.

"I can always find what I want when I don't have anywhere to go," she complained.

"Well, maybe I can find what you need since I don't have a date," I suggested, cooing over a pink-and-blue plaid blouse.

"I think you're enjoying this more than I am," Laurie said.

We bundled into the dressing rooms with a stack of clothes.

"You know, Kevin has never mentioned New Year's to me, but he did ask me if I'd play the piano for him. I said I was too shy," Laurie said, pulling on a pair of white-striped denims. "Paula, I play the piano, but not that well. He's bound to know I'm a fraud if he hears me."

"No, he won't. I never told him I wanted to be a concert pianist. That would have been too much of a hint," I assured her. "Just don't bring up the piano again, and you should be okay."

"I hope it's that easy," Laurie fretted. "Kevin seems nice. . . ."

"I thought so, too." It was good to see Laurie excited about a date, for the first time in months. I watched her madly trying on jeans, finally settling on two pairs: one striped and one plain denim.

"<u>And I</u> *must* have this blouse, and scarf," I said, displaying my choices. "Plus new jeans. At least I'll be well-dressed the next time we go to a movie."

By the time we reached the cosmetics counter, we were toting three bags. Laurie wanted to experiment with perfume, so we emerged from the store smelling like spilled atomizers.

"Let's get a soda," Laurie suggested. "I need to unwind from this shopping blitz."

"Good idea." The Soda Shop was close by, so we went in. Billy Michaelson, a kinky-haired, skinny sophomore we knew from school, was working behind the counter.

He glanced around furtively, making sure no one heard what he had to say to us: "I'm giving you your sodas half-price, because you liven this place up."

Laurie giggled, her face flushed prettily. "What do we do for an encore?" she quipped.

"I forgot my tap shoes," I clowned.

We burst into hysterics. "This must be his standard line reserved for girls who step out of the department store," I joked.

"Oh, no, it isn't!" Billy protested, which made us laugh even harder.

Out on the street, Laurie sniffed her wrists. "I thought we were being followed, but the smell is us."

When I got home, the reaction was much the same from the rest of the family. Dad was lying under the car, fixing something, when I walked through the garage.

"Hi."

"Hi, yourself," he said. "I could smell you a block away."

Mom was sewing a zipper onto an old pair of Meg's pants. She whirled around in her swivel chair when I entered. "What have you been up to?" she asked, sniffing the air.

"Laurie and I were invited to be in a test for a fragrance commercial," I said.

"Really?"

"No, Mom. Just kidding." My mother is so gullible at times. Maybe because she believes just about anything is possible. My father loves to tease her, because she takes him so seriously.

"Mmmm . . . heavenly," Meg said, taking a great whiff of my arm.

"Oh, you're so sweet, Meg." I tickled her. There was no action in the kitchen, which made me wonder. "What's for dinner?"

"We're going out. There are TV dinners for you and Meg," Mom explained.

"I want chili dogs," Meg announced.

"That sounds good. I'll make them," I said, checking to see if we had the ingredients in stock. "Will Regina be out, too?"

"Naturally. When is she ever home on the weekend?"

Staying home on Saturday night was not what I usually did, either. I sighed, tossing the package of hot dogs to Meg. "Well, I guess it's just you and me tonight, Meggie."

"Oh, goodie. Can we make cookies?"

"Sure. Maybe there'll be something good on TV, too."

"Maybe. Can we play Masterpiece, too?"

"Okay. Take full advantage." Masterpiece was Meg's new game, which she was always recruiting players for. I was usually elected, since I enjoy board games.

After everyone left, Meg and I had our dinner and made chocolate chip cookies. Actually, we ate more batter than anything. We shaped the dough into cats, snowmen, and stars.

While we were waiting for each batch to come out of the oven, Meg and I sat together on the piano bench while I played popular songs that she liked. When the cookies were done, we played Masterpiece, then she brought out her paper doll collection.

"These are great," I said, admiring the handmade paper doll clothes.

"Thanks," Meg beamed, and proceeded to show me the whole collection, including some dolls she had made herself.

Sh picked up a dark-haired doll in a long blue gown and began her little story: "This girl is going to a party dressed as Cinderella," she said, propping the cardboard doll against a table leg.

"Is she going in her friend's costume?" I asked, jokingly.

"No, but I guess she could." Meg frowned, considering the idea. "So she meets someone nice, and they dance all night. She's very happy."

They dance all night. . . . A memory of arms around me, moving me across the floor, fluttered in my mind like the warm whisper of his breath against my ear when we'd danced.

After Meg went to bed, I placed her dolls carefully in their shoe box home, reflecting that maybe it wouldn't be half-bad to be a paper doll, instead of human.

I was on Laurie's doorstep early Sunday morning, eager to hear all about her date.

"Come inside. I'll make you a cup of coffee and tell you," Laurie said, letting me in the kitchen door.

"Me, too?" blinked Brad, her fifteen-year-old brother, who was, to Laurie's way of thinking, bratty.

"No, this is not for your ears, Bratty Brad," she said, pouring coffee for the two of us.

"Did it go okay?" I asked, once we were out of Brad's earshot. I would hate to think of Laurie having a bad time. This was all supposed to work out beautifully.

"Oh, it went fine. Kevin is really a nice guy, polite and cute. It's just that . . ." — she seemed pensive — "he mentioned how pretty I, or rather, *we* looked on New Year's."

I was secretly pleased that he mentioned it. "I hope you accepted the compliment gracefully.

"Yes, I did. It just makes me feel a little weird. Like a great imposter," she said.

"It's hard to say which one of us is the imposter," I told Laurie. "I wore your costume to the party, taking your place, and now you're taking mine."

"Yes, but would the Cinderella-and-Prince Charming event have happened if I was wearing the costume and you were home sick?" Laurie posed the question.

"That's something we'll never know the answer to." I shrugged, taking a bite of a sugar donut she offered. "But I bet it would've happened anyway, simply because those two characters go together."

"Still, there are no definite answers to

this." Laurie frowned and took a swallow of coffee.

"Do you think you might fall in love with Kevin?" I asked, gauging Laurie's reaction.

"Isn't it a little early to know?" she laughed. "That was our first date, Paula. And besides, he doesn't know it yet, but he's not really interested in *me*."

"But did he ask you out again?"

"Yes. I'm going to go and hear him play with his band." Her eyes lit up. "And — get this — he wants to find someone for his friend, Stan Kolby."

"Can't Stan find his own date?"

"He's shy and scared. So I suggested you. I said you were a good talker, somebody to pull Stanley out of his shell."

"Might be a little close for comfort," I reflected. "Oh well, the music will be fun, even if the date's a flop."

Laurie tore her jelly donut in two. "I knew you'd want to hear Kevin play. Also it will be nice to have another couple to talk to. Conversation with Kevin is kind of slow at times, but maybe that's because we don't know each other yet."

"Oh, I'm sure that's it, Laurie," I said confidently. "You know how it is getting to know somebody." I knew she would say the same thing if I hesitated about going out with Stan.

"Hmmm."

Just then, Brad barged in with one of his friends, so we had to stop talking.

"Any more donuts left, or did you just leave us the holes?" he joked.

"Actually, we left you crumbs. There's plenty of other food left to inhale, though."

Laurie and I put our coffee cups in the sink, and got ready to go to a matinee. As we got in the car, she turned to me with a devilish grin.

"Well, Paula, back to the subject of Stanley Kolby. It looks like we've attracted not one Prince Charming, but two."

I laughed. "The Lonely Hearts aren't doing too badly," I reflected, and then realized I couldn't remember what Stan Kolby looked like.

Six

Between classes, in the math building, Kevin approached me.

"Did Stan talk to you yet?" he asked.

A poster of several equations in bold print hung above his head. I focused on them, feeling strangely numb. "Uh, no. Should he?"

Kevin blushed. "Yes. I think you should be expecting him to. He's really shy and I thought he'd be better off in a foursome, because it'd be easier to make conversation."

"Isn't he a good friend of yours?" I asked conversationally, pretending I didn't notice how embarrassed he was about this.

"Yes. I guess you could say we're like you and Laurie."

"Sometimes Laurie and I know what each other is going to say next," I said jokingly, although it was partly true.

"Really?" Kevin thrust his hands into his pockets. "I don't think friendships between

53

guys are quite the same as those between girls."

I smiled. "I wouldn't know."

He grinned, then pushed a lock of chestnut hair from his eyes. "See ya' later. Let me know how it goes with Stan."

I watched him stride in the direction of the stairs, feeling all undone with anticipation. Because of Stanley? The thought made me giggle. Honestly, I thought Laurie and I were the mistresses of intrigue with the crazy plans we were always making, but Kevin and Stanley could've run off with the award that week.

Laurie and I were sitting in the cafeteria when I told her about Stan.

"Oh, really?" Laurie looked curious, while forking lasagna into her mouth. "The plot thickens, doesn't it?"

"Yes, well, it would be nice to know the outcome," I grumbled. Somehow, this whole thing had killed my appetite.

"Listen, I've gotta run. Remember, I'm trying out for the part of Ophelia in *Hamlet*." Laurie slid her long legs off the metal seat, scooped up her books and was gone.

"Good luck!" I called after her.

Just as I was ready to sample my lasagna, a shadow fell across my food. I glanced up to behold Stan Kolby (whom I was relieved to recognize) gazing awkwardly down at me.

Stanley was dark-haired, with a thin, waspish face, and a solemn expression which looks joyous when he smiles. Large brown eyes catalog everything with interest, as if he's imagining interviewing you. Stan (as I just remembered), is one of those quiet members of the newspaper staff — the kind who writes poetry but got put in journalism because he can write.

"Hi, Stan. How are you?" I motioned for him to sit down next to me.

His ears turned bright pink. "Just fine, thanks. And you?"

"Fine."

A silence followed. If I'd been chewing food, it would've sounded embarrassingly noisy.

"Uh, I wondered if you might want to double with Kevin and Laurie next weekend," he suggested.

"Sounds like fun," I told him. "What time?"

"Around seven-thirty." Stanley squirmed in his seat. "I'll . . . we'll pick you up, okay?"

"Okay."

On Saturday night, Kevin and Stan came to pick us up at my house. Stan looked neat in a plaid sports jacket and slacks, while Kevin was dressed in new cords and sweater.

My parents treated Laurie and I as though we were both their daughters, and sent us off with the famous last words: "Don't stay out too late now."

"Someone ought to needlepoint those words on a sampler," I said as we trooped down the front steps to Kevin's waiting car.

"That's one of those times when parents

prove themselves to be all alike," Kevin chuckled, opening the door for Laurie and me.

For an instant, as Laurie scrambled into the car, Kevin's dark brown eyes met mine. A confusing warmth spread out from the pit of my stomach. I looked away.

Once we were on our way, Kevin asked Laurie about the audition.

"I'll find out Monday if I got the part," she said.

"What part did you try out for, Laurie?" Stan questioned. He was bent over like a question mark in the backseat of Kevin's little car.

"Ophelia. I think it would be a fun part to do because it's so dramatic." Laurie pressed a bright purple cloche hat over her reddish-gold mane.

I asked Stan what he was working on for the paper lately.

"I'm starting a poetry page. If you know of anyone who might like to submit, let them know, okay?" he told us.

Combo's was a small, shack-like building set back from the main route. The parking lot was full of potholes, which we had to dodge to get to the front entrance.

"This place isn't very glamorous, but it's a lot of fun," Kevin explained, leading the way.

We chose a table close to the stage, so that we would have the best view. Laurie and Stan sat down, while Kevin and I went to get drinks, because we were in the middle of a conversation about music.

"This music is really different from what we do in class, of course, but I love it. With a band, you can try out so many different things — blues, rock with traditional rhythms like calypso. And everybody brings something new to the performance."

"Sounds like a lot of fun," I said. We stood at the bar. Kevin handed me two sodas, for Stan and me.

We walked back to our table, and passed the drinks around.

"Well, see ya' after the show." Kevin smiled, and toasted all of us.

"To a great show." Stan raised his glass, and Kevin stepped up on stage.

Roy Redman, the drummer, was a frizzy-haired, plump boy who played in Kevin's band. Gus Wiseman was the bass player — tall, angular, with short black hair and the beginnings of a mustache. There was a piano, but no piano player, so I envisioned myself on the empty stool.

I sat down next to Stan and Laurie, who were already involved in a conversation about the school newspaper. I never knew Laurie was interested in it, but she seemed to be hanging on every word Stan said. It turned my attention to the band, who moved into their first rollicking number with great enthusiasm.

The music zoomed through my limbs, and when that first song was over, the crowd applauded wildly. But Kevin didn't wait for a response; he just took their energy and moved right into the next number, a calypso with a gentle, pulsing rhythm that put a little sway to me. I wished I could get up and dance.

Kevin was a great performer. He leaned casually against the piano, lifted the sax to his lips and rocked with the music. The notes rippled down like melted butter, coating me. He closed his eyes on some notes, and the concentration during difficult passages was etched on his face — poised, waiting, until each sound reached its zenith.

He was in complete control, and yet completely moved by his music. I recognized that feeling — the elevated sensation you got from either playing or listening.

I looked over at Laurie. "Why didn't we ever come here before?" I asked her.

"I don't think it gets enough advertising," she answered. Her eyes shone in the dim light, which I took to mean she'd fallen madly in love with Kevin. But then I noticed Stan studying her profile, while he sat next to me.

The Lonely Hearts were doing okay, I decided, as Kevin stepped down for a break. We were both having fun, and I hadn't seen that look in Laurie's eyes since Don had left for California.

Kevin took the empty seat between Laurie and me. "So how'd you like it?" he asked, grinning from ear to ear.

"Oh, it was wonderful," I breathed, in unison with everyone else.

"You're fantastic," Laurie said.

"Really different from orchestra, Kevin," I commented.

"This is what I call 'free expression,' " he explained.

"Or what Stan calls, 'letting it all hang out,' " Stan added, and we all laughed.

Stanley ordered more sodas and a plate of brownies, while we talked. A pretty red-headed girl came to our table to compliment Kevin.

"Loved that last song, Kev," she said. Obviously, she knew him pretty well.

He took the compliment graciously, while a shaft of memory pierced me. The girl reminded me of all the girls who hung around Ricky after the games. After awhile, I wondered if they simply like to be in the glow of other people's success.

Kevin's hand accidentally brushed against mine. I glanced up and met his gaze, trembling inside. He offered me a one-sided smile, and I found myself smiling back.

"I really liked that last song, too, Kevin," I told him.

"Really? Another homemade one," he said modestly.

"I've never tried composing," I said. "Do you ever write words to your music?"

"Not yet, but I've been thinking about it."

We turned our attention to Laurie and

Stan, who were talking about Hamlet. Their heads were inclined across the table, nearly touching, and illuminated by the lit candle behind them.

"Sounds like you two have the Bard on the Brain," I joked, and Stan and Laurie looked up, Stan turning bright red. Kevin and I laughed.

Then Kevin brought over the band members and introduced us. Roy and Gus gobbled down a couple of brownies, and then told Kevin it was time to get back to work.

"See you later," Kevin said, leaping agilely up on stage.

"Nice meeting you," chimed Gus and Roy, following Kevin.

I watched Kevin lean into his music, then pull back, his fingers dancing over the sax's pads with fluttering precision. Then I studied Laurie's and Stan's rapt faces, and I felt filled with a strange contentment. It was very pleasant being out with Stan and Kevin. Stan didn't annoy me or demand too much from me. In fact, Laurie had talked to him for most of the evening, leaving me free to listen to the music or talk to Kevin about it.

I had to admit that I did enjoy discussing music with him, and I was intrigued by his composing. There had always been so many pieces I wanted to learn on the piano, that I'd never even thought of writing any of my own.

The lights dimmed for the last number, softening the room with a romantic feeling.

Couples moved closer together, and warmth enveloped me as the music wove its haunting rhythm throughout the room. Kevin's gaze rested on our table, and we all smiled up at him, nodding our encouragement. And when the last, long, melancholy note died in Combo's, the applause and cheers took over in a near-deafening salute.

After that response, the band members were pretty excited. We all sat down together after Combo's emptied for the evening, talking music.

"How long have you been playing the piano, Paula?" Stan asked me.

"Since my feet could reach the pedals," I told him, and everyone laughed. "I used to pound on the piano so much, I think my parents just gave in and decided to give me lessons."

"You should hear Paula play sometime," Kevin told the band. "She's very good."

I could feel the heat rising into my cheeks, as both Laurie and Stan reaffirmed what Kevin said about me.

"I hate to break up this happy party, but we did promise to get you two girls home early," Kevin reminded us. "The last thing I want is two sets of unhappy parents."

Laurie and I groaned simultaneously. We said good-night to Roy and Gus, and went out to the car.

On the way home, sitting next to Stan, I hummed a bar from one of the tunes Kevin played.

"Sounds like you enjoyed yourself," Stan said to me, grinning.

"I did. Thanks for taking me," I told him. "I would've hated to miss such a good time."

He smiled, and I thought about what a nice guy he was. Although we didn't really talk that much, I felt pretty comfortable with him. He wasn't a Ricky-type, that was for sure, so I could feel safe.

We dropped Laurie off first. Kevin kissed her lightly on the cheek before she slid out of the car. I felt a slight pang and wondered if Stan would kiss me when we got to my house, but he didn't.

Instead, he squeezed my hand through his glove. "Good-night, Paula. I had fun. See you in school," he said.

"See you, Stanley," I said, scooting across the cold vinyl seat. "See you, Kevin."

They both waved as I trekked up the walk, while I was wondering if Stan would ask me out again. The evening had been so much fun that he might want to double again. And for me, being with Laurie helped, too. Together, we could fill in any lulls in conversation.

But for some reason, as Kevin's car disappeared down the road, a puzzle of feelings overtook me. Maybe the music caused it, I decided. Kevin's music was the kind that leaves you with strange feelings of warmth, openness, and longing.

Quickly, I undressed and climbed under the quilt, wondering if Laurie and Kevin would go out together again, and if Stan and I would, and did Kevin really admire my playing, as I admired his?

At last, I fell asleep, after telling myself that I'd just have to stay tuned for the answers to these, and many more, of my questions.

Seven

"We've been invited to Stanley's hockey game tomorrow after school," Laurie told me on the way to school Monday morning.

I was studying madly for a chem quiz while she drove. "Oh? Do I get a personal invitation, or do all mine come from Stan via you?" I asked. I could just imagine shy Stan asking Kevin to ask Laurie to ask me out.

"You probably will. I'm just preparing you."

"It seems like someone's always warning me about Stanley's upcoming invitations," I observed. "Are you going?"

"Yes. Kevin says Stan's a great player. I wouldn't miss it for the world," she giggled. Then I remembered that although my interest in sports was pretty minimal, Laurie loved ice skating and probably hockey, too.

"Sounds like fun," I said, as she parked

against a drift, and we got out of the car. It was snowing hard. Big fluffy flakes swirled around us as we trekked across the slippery pavement to the main building. "Just in case I don't get my personal invite, find out what time we'll be getting home, will you? I've got a lot to do this week, with the orchestra concert coming up this weekend," I reminded Laurie.

"Oh, sure. I understand," she said, watching her footing on the icy steps. "I've got a quiz in art history to study for, too."

We said good-bye as we went our separate ways toward our morning classes. In first period, an announcement was made that we would have an assembly third period, to see an educational film entitled *Cross Section of America*. I was ecstatic, because it meant I'd miss geometry, my least favorite class.

Stanley and I ran into each other in a row of folding chairs in the auditorium. He looked embarrassed when he realized it was me, and pulled nervously at his Adam's apple.

"Uh, hi, Paula. Did you hear about the hockey game?" he asked.

"Yes, I got your invitation through the grapevine. Thank you, Stanley," I teased, making him blush even more deeply.

"I was going to call you. . . ." he stumbled over an explanation.

"I know, just teasing. Yes, I'd love to go, but I have to be home early. I have an orchestra concert coming up this weekend."

"Sure. I know, Kevin has that, too." Shifting from one foot to the other, he finally said, "Well, I have to go. My class is over there." He pointed toward the side exit. "Nice seeing you."

"Same here." I watched him join his class, and sit down next to Kevin. Kevin's profile was so unlike Stan's — just like their personalities. Much like Laurie and me, I decided, glancing over in that direction when the lights went out.

Students clapped in the darkness, and then the light from the projector threw a wide beam across the room. I turned my attention to the film, which was about teenage activities and customs in different cities across America.

A Chicago high-rise came into view, and a picture of teens playing basketball in a concrete schoolyard. A thought of Kevin on stage flashed through my mind . . . of him looking down at me. Did he have any idea I was the one he kissed New Year's Eve? Of course not — that was my secret. And it was probably just because I hadn't kissed anyone in months that the moment stuck in my mind.

I pushed that thought away to concentrate on a shot of a large group of 4-Hers showing their livestock at a county fair in Iowa. That scene was followed by surfers in California, and then a high school class in Tucson, Arizona on an archeological dig, uncovering ancient Indian pottery.

After the film, as we filed out, I noticed

Kevin and Stan up ahead, talking, and then I remembered that my next class was orchestra. Once outside, I cut out of line and hurried straight across the quad to the music room. The wind was blowing snow into icy sheets that hit my face like little needles. Already during the morning, three inches had fallen, forming a crisp, new layer over the school.

Someone tapped me on the shoulder just as I started into the music building. I whirled to face Kevin.

"Going my way?" He grinned, the wind tugging his hair into stiff peaks.

"Oh, yeah," I mumbled, surprised to see him. "How's your practicing for the concert coming along?"

"Pretty good. As long as I don't think about it too much in advance, I'm fine." He held the door of the room open for me, but kept talking.

"I hear we're going to a hockey game tomorrow," I said.

Kevin chuckled. "So you heard? I wonderd when Stan would get around to asking you."

Mr. McEllis, our orchestra teacher, walked over to talk to Kevin. He was a slight, balding man with compassionate gray eyes. I always felt as though I was in good hands under his direction, because he was an excellent teacher and conductor.

We exchanged hellos and I went over to the piano. My stomach was knotted up, and

I couldn't figure out why. Just before we started practice, I glanced over at Kevin, and he winked at me.

Then, when we began to play, with Mr. McEllis urging us, pulling us along, my nervousness unraveled in the sweetness of our harmony.

Kevin, Stan, Laurie, and I gathered at my house before going to Stan's ice hockey game. Stan looked the most excited I'd ever seen him. There was a definite twinkle in his eyes.

While we waited for Laurie to arrive (we planned to go in two cars, in case I had to leave early), I offered the boys Cokes in the kitchen. Stan declined, asking if he could please have orange juice or water.

"You know these jocks, Paula. They only eat health stuff," Kevin joked.

I bristled, recalling Ricky, who was a jock, but not a health food-nut, by any means. He was a hamburger-, pizza-, and soft drink-nut. For a moment, I thought maybe Kevin's remark was aimed at the fact that I used to date Ricky, but then I decided I was probably being overly sensitive. He probably knew nothing about Ricky.

"I've known lots of jocks," I said slowly, "but not all of them have been health food-nuts."

"I think I hear Laurie's car." Stan leaned in the direction of the driveway, where the soft rumble of a motor grew louder, then quiet.

"Oh, hi, Cinderella," Kevin said, as my little sister entered the kitchen, decked out in the Cinderella wig and an elaborate blue chiffon party dress.

"Hi, Kevin. How did you recognize me?" she teased, curtseying graciously.

"*Meg*," I gasped, my hand flying to cover my mouth.

Kevin's gaze shifted from me to Meg. "Well, it seems that I've run into Cinderella recently, so I'm quite familiar with her."

It was taking every ounce of my willpower not to react to this situation. "More Coke, Kevin?" I asked mildly.

"Oh, no, thanks, Paula," he replied, reaching out to touch the stiff wig. "What I'm wondering, is, where'd you get that wig?"

His coffee-brown eyes seemed to see right through me. I hope he didn't notice me trembling. "Uh, we borrowed the wig from Laurie, didn't we, Meg?"

"Well, *you* did," she answered frankly. I could've killed her. Why hadn't I told her the whole story so she would go along with me on this?

"No, uh . . . Laurie left it here after the party," I started to explain shakily. I hated to lie. My parents always said they could tell when I lied because there was a slight twitch under one of my eyes when I faced them. Well, I could feel the twitch now, working away, and I was just glad Kevin didn't know this about me.

Just then, Stan opened the kitchen door to let Laurie in.

"Hi, gang!" she called cheerily, distracting Kevin from the Cinderella wig, which Meg danced off with. I noticed Laurie watch her leave, but she didn't say anything. She glanced at me for a reaction.

Kevin was watching, so I couldn't give Laurie any sort of look to let her know what was going on.

"Did you know your Cinderella wig was here?" Kevin quizzed Laurie.

"Uh, yes. I realized it when I went to take the costume back to the drama department at the college," Laurie told him, as casually as she could muster.

I breathed a silent sigh of relief. We made it through that one, but I had the feeling, from the way Kevin kept watching me the rest of the afternoon, that he was suspicious.

By the time we got to the arena where Stan's game was being held, I felt relaxed. I was surprised to see that Stan played forward brilliantly. Somehow, I always thought of him as big and clumsy, but he was very quick and agile on skates. He even looked transformed once he changed into his gray-and-blue uniform, with shoulder and knee pads.

It was a playoff game against the Tigers from Terrence High School, across town. The Beecher Lions had played their last two games well, and were doing great during the first period of this one.

If it hadn't been for Laurie, however, pointing out all Stan's glowing moves, I probably wouldn't have become so excited.

"Look at Stanley!" she squealed, as Stan and Ken Torrey battled over a position, locking their sticks together. Finally, Stan broke free and got to the puck, only to be knocked from behind by Ken and sent sprawling flat on his face. Several other players piled on top of him, and I sat there and winced, imagining how Stan must feel under that pile of sweaty bodies.

The blast of the referee's whistle put an end to Stanley's torture, and presented the Tigers with a penalty. Kevin's eyes rested on me when I turned to see Laurie's reaction. He kept staring, until I felt my palms grow sweaty, and I pushed them into the pockets of my down jacket, then quickly looked away. *Why does he have to keep looking at me?* I wondered, in frustration. There was no way I was going to like him, but he was showing a lot of interest in me now — ever since Meg brandished the silly Cinderella wig in front of his face. When I get my hands on her, I'll. . . .

Just then, Laurie leaped to her feet and screamed, "Go Stanley!" Stanley and defenseman Terry Todd were passing the puck back and forth, headed for the goal. The score was three to two, Lions' favor. My hands formed fists as Rhett Whitney of the opposition cut in front of Terry and lifted the puck right up and out of his reach. Sam Steinberg of the Tigers was on the receiving end, hightailing it down the ice to shoot it straight into the goal, bringing the score up to three to three.

The Tigers cheering section erupted in wild screams and applause. Stan and Terry Todd exchanged mischievous grins, which I hoped the opposition didn't notice. Laurie leaned forward on the hard bleacher bench, her lips parted, eyes shining in anticipation of Stan's next move. I never knew she was so interested in hockey before this. Or maybe it was that she was interested in Stan. *Could that be it?* I wondered.

The game had gone into sudden-death overtime. Breaking free of the defense, Stan took the puck down the ice, a cluster of players hot on his tail, but when one started to crowd him, he shot the black rubber puck over to Terry. Ed Casey, a Tiger defenseman, intercepted it, then pushed forward through a tangle of sticks to the open ice, heading back the way they'd come. Stan was right behind him, his expression going ashen as the puck flew toward the Tiger's goal, as though heaven and earth couldn't stop it.

But Willis Carson, goalie, did. There was a sudden, ear-splitting crack as his hockey stick met the puck and sent it skittering across the ice, into perfect position for Stan to take it. There were only seconds left in the game. Skate blades flashed as players skidded to catch up, intent on not letting Stanley make a goal.

The entire audience was on its feet, screaming so loudly I thought their lungs would burst, stamping their feet as the Tigers again tried to intercept Stanley as he glided toward the net. Yet he deftly sent the puck over to Terry, who was almost instantly surrounded by fire-breathing Tigers. So Terry whacked it back to Stan, and Stan, with the coast now clear, shot the puck into the air, out of reach of the frustrated, flailing goalie, dead-center into the net.

A new number flashed on the scoreboard — four to three, our favor — just as the horn ending the game sounded. The Lions had won the game!

Kids everywhere jumped up and down, hugging each other. Laurie grabbed me, as she screamed in my ear, "Wow! Did you see that?" Excitement was bursting out of every pore.

Kevin laughed and started to walk down the bleachers, his hands shoved deep in his pockets, his breath turned to mist in the chill air. "C'mon, let's see how Stan's faring after his victory," he suggested, motioning to Laurie and me.

But his eyes, the color of coffee, locked with mine, not Laurie's, and I was filled with an overwhelming giddiness. Laurie was chattering nonstop about how wonderful Stanley had been, and in the distant recesses of my brain I could hear her carrying on, and myself nodding in response, but not really listening. And Kevin wasn't saying anything, just looking at me, the corners of his lips suddenly, cautiously, moving upward into a smile.

Then the three of us shouldered our way through the crush of people, all talking exuberantly about the game, to where Stan stood, wiping his perspiring face with an old gym towel. `

He was surrounded by team members, all wearing ear-splitting grins.

"Fabulous, just fabulous." Kevin slapped Stan on the back. "You're headed for stardom. That was some expert shot you placed there at the finish. I'm surprised these guys aren't kissing your feet."

Stan's grin widened. "I think they're waiting until I take my shower," he said in a low voice, which caused Kevin to toss his head back in laughter.

"Stan, you were great," Laurie greeted him. There was admiration in her eyes.

"Great game, Stan," I nodded in agreement, but Laurie was still gazing at him with a goofy look on her face. What was with her, lately?

"Thanks, everybody," Stan said, wadding up his towel. "Hey, listen, I'm starved after all this exercise. Let me clean up, and maybe we can all get something to eat."

I couldn't remember Stan talking this much before, but maybe excitement loosened his tongue. "I've got to study," I hedged, thinking of the mound of work I had to accomplish this week, in addition to practicing for the concert.

Kevin nudged me. "Hey, come on, Paula. It's not every day Stan's a hero, and it's still early enough to get a snack, and be home before dinner. How about it?"

"Oh, okay," I said. "You talked me into it."

"Since when did you ever pass up an opportunity to eat?" Laurie asked me.

Her comment sparkèd a pleased smile from Kevin.

"For your information," I returned, "since I've been thinking about playing piano in front of the entire student body. I don't want to make my debut as a blimp."

Kevin chuckled, but his tone was soothing when he said to me, "Don't worry, Paula. I know you'll play beautifully, and look great."

His compliment warmed me, all the way to The Soda Shop. It was one of those cutesy little ice-cream parlors done in pink-and-white stripes, with metal chairs and tables. We all ordered hamburgers — Stanley ordered five just for himself.

"I guess playing hockey works up quite an appetite," I commented, since I was sitting beside him, watching him carefully squeeze ketchup and mustard on each patty.

He blushed redder than the ketchup. "Well, yeah. I usually eat a lot after practice and games," he explained. He was perched on one of the shop's dainty metal chairs, which made him look huge. I had to keep myself from giggling at the sight.

A few kids who'd watched the game trailed in and came by to compliment Stan, but he found it hard to respond to praise with his mouth full.

Obviously, Kevin thought it was funny, because to one girl, Willa Perry, he said, "Stanley wishes to thank you for your lovely compliments, but he is unable to personally reply at the moment."

To which Stanley shot him a dark glance, sending us all into gales of laughter.

Then he and Laurie started talking about the game, and Kevin turned to me. "I love the Gershwin solo you're working on for the concert," he said. "Is that going easy for you?"

"Pretty much so. I love it, too, which makes it much easier to play. And it's not too complicated," I explained. "Are you playing some of your own work?"

"Just one piece," he said. The deepening shadows of late afternoon cast a faint, shimmering light over his features, emphasizing his strong cheekbones. "I haven't decided on which one, yet."

"Do you choose according to mood?" I asked, thinking that if I wrote music, I would do that — if Mr. McEllis allowed it.

Kevin grinned. "Probably I will, which means I have to practice every piece. Or think up something new." He was silent a moment. "I've been thinking about writing about a recent inspiration. I might call it 'The Cinderella Song.' " He regarded me with amusement, waiting for my response.

"Sounds good," I replied blandly, while fear fluttered in my heart. I had a sudden urge to join the conversation next to us, about hockey, so I turned to listen in.

". . . been playing ever since I was a freshman, and I've been approached by a couple college teams," Stanley was saying.

"Really?" Laurie's blue eyes were admiring.

"I'm not sure where I want to go to college, yet, though," Stan went on. "But I do know I want to major in physical education . . . or maybe drama," he smiled at Laurie.

"Why, Stan, I didn't know you were interested in drama," she cried in obvious delight.

"Well, maybe just since I've been talking to you," he cleared his throat nervously, and we all laughed.

Was Laurie really responsible for inspiring Stan about drama? I wondered. It was true that they spend a good deal of time talking about her role in *Hamlet*, and past productions.

Laurie's sudden — or growing, I wasn't sure which — interest in Stanley Kolby was not helping things. This wasn't part of the plan. Besides, I didn't like the way Kevin was looking at me lately. He was supposed to be falling madly in love with Laurie, and not noticing me at all. I was only her best friend.

We waited patiently for Stan to finish eating, since his order was by far the largest, and spent the time talking about the game. Finally, there were only a few fries left on his plate, and not much more to say, so we left.

Outside The Soda Shop, we all said goodbye and piled into our own cars. Of course, once we were on the road, Laurie quizzed me about Stan.

"What do you think of Stan?" she asked.

I took a deep breath, shrugging nonchalantly. "Well, I've never seen anyone devour five hamburgers in a row before. I mean, I've read about these marathon eaters in the *Guinness Book of World Records*, but. . . ."

Laurie interrupted. "But what else? Don't you think he is a great hockey player?"

"Oh, yeah, sure. He's kind of cute in his own way, too."

"Well, I think he's cute, and so talented," she oozed, which was not what I wanted to hear.

Personally, I wasn't bowled over by Stan. He wasn't magical to me. He didn't make the skin on my neck ripple deliciously. He didn't cause a smile to start on my face the minute I saw him — but I didn't tell Laurie those things. The people who caused that kind of reaction in me were the kind who broke my heart, anyway, so it was probably better not to bring it up. Actually, the fact that Stanley triggered absolutely *no* reaction in me was what I liked about him. It meant I was safe with him. I wouldn't fall for him. I could go out with him, laugh and have a good time, and look forward to a dreamless sleep.

We were almost to my house when Laurie spoke to me again. Usually, she talks a lot more, but I think she exhausted her vocal chords on Stan.

"Paula," she began quietly, "didn't you see how Kevin was looking at you today?"

"If he was, it's only because Meg dragged out that stupid Cinderella wig and confused him," I replied. "Everything was going according to plan up until then."

"I'm sure that isn't the only reason," she said. "I'll bet that wig only brought to a head a whole bunch of his suspicions. I just wish you'd tell him the truth."

"What for?"

"Because he likes you, not me. You're Cinderella, and every time he looks at *me*, I get the feeling he's real disappointed."

She pulled into my driveway. One of my favorite Lionel Richie songs was on the radio, and I hummed a bit before answering her.

"If he is, he's an idiot, Laurie," I responded flatly. "I'm not interested in him, so there's no sense in him knowing that *I'm* Cinderella."

Laurie sighed wearily. "Okay, if you say

so, but he knows something's up. And I don't know how long we can go on playing this charade."

Her words struck a chord of fear in me. All the evidence, except for the foul up with Meg and the wig, had pointed to Laurie as Cinderella, so I felt entirely safe in my lie ... up until now. But even the wig was easily explained, and in my mind, no Prince Charming was going to question such a solid explanation as Kevin had received from Laurie.

"Look, Cinderella," I said calmly, "just consider this another part you're playing. You're an excellent actress, and so far, you've had a flawless career. Now this might be one of your shining moments."

She giggled nervously. "I sure hope so."

I trudged up the path to my house, burdened with the unsettling thought that a thin line existed between fantasy and reality — too thin a line.

E^{ight}

"Help! Laurie, my hair!" I wailed, holding my hair by the ends to demonstrate how unruly it was. The image in my vanity mirror was one of sheer frustration.

Laurie was helping me get ready for the orchestra concert tonight.

"No one said this sophisticated look was going to come easy," she pointed out. "Of course, you've got the basics: good looks, nice hair. . . ."

I wanted my hair twisted up in a soft bun for my piano solo. The whole school would be watching, and I had to make a spectacular presentation.

Laurie wound my hair around her fingers, expertly pinning it into an attractive twist. Then she combed the feathered bangs forward and used the curling iron on them.

"Now, how do you like that?" she asked, standing back to admire her handiwork.

"I love it!" I exclaimed, examining the hairdo from every angle in my mother-of-pearl mirror. "You've transformed me!"

"I'll bet Kevin isn't going through all this for his performance," Laurie commented dryly.

"Well, maybe he doesn't have to go through as much effort to look great. Still, I think boys do worry about how they look." Even before she said anything more, I was thinking about how Ricky used to gaze at himself in the mirror. I should've known by his narcissistic streak that he wasn't for me.

"Remember," Laurie reflected, "Ricky was the vainest of them all."

We giggled, but I always got a bitter taste in my mouth at the thought of him, even though my feelings for him had dulled quite a bit. The worst part now was judging everything that happened in my life according to what happened with Ricky — such as Kevin. But I also figured that Ricky was a lesson, a painful one, to teach me never to get involved with guys like him again. So, in a way, he had saved me from a lot of hassles. I already knew what I had to do when Kevin came along — no matter what Laurie said . . . or thought.

Believe it or not, she was still thinking I should tell Kevin the truth, but she wasn't saying so, because she knew it would make me nervous. And the last thing I needed just before the performance was to be made nervous!

I wore a black velvet dress, with two gold chains around my neck, and lacey black panty hose. Once, I'd seen a pianist wearing a long, flowing black dress. She glided onto the stage, the picture of elegance, before sitting down to electrify everyone in the audience.

Since then, I vowed I would have that kind of outfit, and try to attain the kind of presence that pianist had. My dress hit me just below the knee, because it was a more practical length for me, but it was still flowing, black, and elegant.

"You look beautiful," Laurie admired me, looking very pleased. She wore a soft, kitten-gray angora sweater and matching plaid skirt. I thought Kevin would like that outfit. The only trouble was, Laurie had to leave right after the performance because she had a babysitting job, so they wouldn't be able to go out together.

"All set?" Mom, Dad, and Regina watched Laurie and I descend the stairs.

My father wolf-whistled. "Wow, do you look . . . different, Paula. Very glamorous."

"Thanks, Dad. A lot of effort went into this, you realize. I'd like to thank my wardrobe consultant and hairstylist, Laurie Wellington." I stepped aside so Laurie could take a bow.

My family clapped, complimented Laurie on her fine work, and then we filed out to the car. No one complained about being squashed together so tightly in the car — it was seventeen degrees outside. I was glad to have my full-length down coat, since the black dress was lovely but not warm.

As Dad pulled the car out into the road, the headlights swung across a new snowfall, revealing a startled doe, poised by the shed on the side of our house. Her eyes looked fiery red as the light hit them, a moment before she bounded into the close webbing of trees almost as quickly as she had appeared.

I held my hands in my lap, rubbing them together to keep them warm for the performance. In my mind, I replayed the notes I would play later, and imagined how the music would sound drifting across the auditorium. I had practiced for so long and hard that each passage was now a part of me.

My parents let me off at the backstage entrance. Excitement met me at the door, where the intent faces of orchestra members gathered to see who had arrived. Everyone was hastily putting the last minute touches on their outfits, or tuning up their instruments.

"You look smashing," Carol Wilson, another flutist, complimented me.

"Thanks," I said.

"I think the boys look great in dark pants and white shirts, don't you?" she said, an impish glint in her smoke-gray eyes.

"Yes, and especially with bow ties," I giggled.

"Is this our star pianist?" I spun around at the sound of Kevin's deep voice. He looked particularly handsome in his white ruffled shirt and bow tie, his chestnut hair slicked back, the comb tracks still visible.

"Save the flattery until I prove myself, Kevin," I replied, a new surge of jitters rising up in me.

"That shouldn't be too hard for you, Paula," he said, smiling warmly.

For some reason, talking to Kevin made me nervous. I needed to talk to Mr. McEllis, to get my pep talk before going on. "It's sweet of you to say so," I told Kevin, quickly changing the subject. "Will you excuse me? I need to find Mr. McEllis."

"He's right over there." Kevin pointed me in the direction of the water cooler, where the teacher usually hangs out before a performance.

Beads of perspiration stood out on Mr. McEllis's forehead, but his expression lit up when he saw me. "Ah, Paula, don't worry, pet. I've got all the confidence in the world, in you. You're the best."

I breathed a sigh of relief. "I just knew I could count on you to say the words I had to hear," I told him gratefully, and he squeezed my hand.

The orchestra filed on stage. A few minutes of tuning followed, and the audience grew silent. Mr. McEllis made an announcement, cracked a few jokes (the same ones he told every year), and then we began.

We played the *Star Wars* medley for openers, and then another mix of popular songs.

The orchestra as a whole was doing well, and the audience applauded appreciatively.

Then it was my turn to perform a Gershwin solo. I heard a certain segment of the audience clap when Mr. McEllis announced me, which triggered applause all around. I sat up straight, took a deep breath — my fingers poised over the keys — then began to play.

Summertime rippled over the silence like a mountain stream, and I moved along with it. The music flowed beneath my skin and resounded in my heart. I was concentrating, but I was also absorbed. The earthy tones flooded into the auditorium, and hung suspended by invisible strands, while fresh ones climbed over them.

The music was an imaginary finger on my spine, tracing my emotions, until the last note faded into deep quiet.

The quiet stretched, and I wondered if the audience would respond, when the first applause cracked the air.

My hands dropped into my lap, tingling. I rose to accept the thundering applause, which was coming from the orchestra, too. Then I spotted my parents, Regina, Meg, and Laurie, all looking jubilant. Behind me, I heard Kevin yell, "Bravo!", sending a tingle down my spine.

Finally, the auditorium grew quiet again, and Kevin stepped up to the microphone with his flute. He raised the instrument to his lips, and a long, quivering note filled the room, then moved into a lilting rhythm which made me want to dance around the stage.

The presence of Kevin's music commanded rapt attention, reflected on the faces in the audience. When he finished playing, the crowd went wild, and so did the orchestra. I shouted "bravo" to him, and he turned slightly, in the middle of a bow, and winked at me.

Excitement rippled through me. For an instant, I felt connected to Kevin, perhaps because we shared an appreciation of each other's performance.

The audience demanded an encore, so the orchestra struck up a rollicking Elton John song, to which everyone clapped in time to the music.

When it was over, Kevin came over to me. His eyes were shining. "Congratulations, Paula. You were really wonderful out there."

"Thank you, Kevin. So were you. The flute piece was fantastic. You are a great composer," I told him.

His ears turned pink, and I could tell he was pleased with the compliment. Suddenly Laurie, Stan, and his cousin, Angie, were at our side, soon followed by my family. Laurie hugged me hard, bubbling with congratulations.

Stan left a light kiss on my cheek. "Boy, you two are fabulous," he said. "Can I have your autographs?"

"Oh, Paula, we're so proud of you," Mom and Dad gushed, hugging me. "You were just wonderful. . . ."

"Next stop, Carnegie Hall," Regina said as she leaned over to kiss me.

"What's Carnegie Hall?" Meg piped up, and everyone laughed.

Stan introduced his cousin, Angie. "You were very good," she complimented us in her whispery voice. She was tall, with short, honey-blonde hair and blue-gray eyes.

"Thanks." Kevin and I looked at each other and grinned excitedly.

"Well, what do we do now?" I asked everybody.

"You know that we have dinner to go to at the Hillstroms'," my mother told me.

"And I've got a date," Regina said.

"I've got to babysit," Laurie added, slipping into her coat.

Kevin looked from me to Stan and Angie. "Well, I planned on going out after this to celebrate."

Stan cleared his throat. "Well, would you like to go out, Paula?" he asked.

"I'd love to," I said.

A short, delicate looking woman with black hair approached us. Kevin put an arm around her. "This is my mother, Dorothy Stevens," he said, then turned to me. "And this is the wonderful pianist you heard tonight, Paula Rizzoni."

I turned crimson, but Mrs. Stevens was

delighted to shake my hand. "Oh, you were great, Paula. I loved it."

"Thank you."

"If you will excuse me, I have a business meeting I must get to," Mrs. Stevens explained. "But it was nice meeting you all."

We exchanged good-byes. Then my father said they'd better get going, or they would be unfashionably late.

"Have fun!" my parents called.

"Don't celebrate too hard!" Reggie warned with the shaking of a finger. Meg wanted to know just who she was going to end up with, so Reggie took her in hand and explained that, unfortunately, she would have a sitter tonight.

Kevin scooped a lock of hair from his eyes, offering me a half smile. "Let's go celebrate. C'mon, Paula, just look at those stars in your eyes!"

"What?" I blinked, and Stan, Kevin, and Angie started laughing.

Nine

We made plans to meet the rest of the orchestra at a place called the Rendezvous.

Kevin put a hand on my shoulder, startling me. "I'll go warm up the car. Meet you in the parking lot, okay?"

"Okay." I slipped on my coat, and Stan, Angie, and I waded through the crowded auditorium, hearing praise on all sides. It was wonderful. I was certain fame would agree with me — even recognition would do.

Once we were outside, Stan turned to me and said, "Angie and I will meet you there, okay?"

For a moment, I was puzzled, but then one glance at his two-seater sports car explained why he didn't ask me to join them. So I crunched over the ice to Kevin's car and climbed in.

"Mmmm. It's toasty in here," I said, curling into the seat.

"Comfortable?" He smiled at me.

"Yes, very." I felt a little strange being left with Kevin, but he acted as though he thought it was the most natural thing on earth.

Kevin drove out onto the state route. The woods flashed by in their deep, snowy, splendor, tree branches drooping wearily from weight. The road wound up the mountainside, a glistening wet ribbon under moonlight. It was a very romantic scene, and I thought Laurie should be with Kevin to enjoy it.

"It's too bad Laurie couldn't come tonight," I said.

"Yeah." Kevin didn't take his eyss off the road, so I kept talking.

"She really wanted to, I think. Didn't she look nice tonight?"

"She always looks nice."

"But especially tonight," I insisted. Kevin remained quiet. "Did you know that Laurie is also a good singer, besides an actress?"

"I think you mentioned it before."

Did I? "Well, it doesn't hurt to repeat it," I said defensively.

"What are your plans for the future, Paula?" he asked.

I got the feeling Kevin wanted to change the subject. "I plan to be a concert pianist."

He smiled. "You're pretty ambitious, aren't you?"

"Yes." I grinned. "That's the only way to get what you want."

"Very true."

"What about you?"

"I'm not sure exactly what area I'll settle on yet, but you can bet it will be musical."

The Rendezvous swung into view, a blaze of bright lights coming from an unobtrusive, flat-roofed building set apart from a row of shops. Stan pulled into the parking area just as Kevin and I got out of the car. The muffled sounds of a party in progress could be heard across the lot.

"Sounds like a good time!" Kevin said as we entered the room.

A gust of warm air and food aromas assaulted us as we walked in the door. Stan walked between Angie and I, which looked a little funny, while Kevin strode ahead of us.

"Maybe some night you can hear Kevin's band play, Angie," I suggested to the shy girl.

"Oh, I'd love to. I'll be here for another week," she told me, once we'd selected a cozy booth in a corner of the restaurant. Stan and Kevin went to get our orders.

"Stan tells me you're visiting from California," I said.

"Uh, yes. Funny time of the year to visit, isn't it?" Angie giggled. She seemed very nice.

"Not if you like snow, or skiing."

The food and the boys arrived. The Rendezvous makes about the greatest pizza in town, so we ordered a big combination pie.

Stan and Kevin devoured three slices in the time it took Angie and I to eat one. Between bites, we discussed hockey, music, movies, and Laurie's upcoming part in *Hamlet*.

And then, about that time, Angie started to turn green.

"Angie, are you all right?" I questioned. She was holding her stomach and making a very funny face.

"Actually, Paula, I'm not. My stomach's really upset all of a sudden," she said, her voice growing even more shadowy than it was naturally. "Maybe the plane ride and the rich food have something to do with it."

"Oh, it's probably a combination of all those things, plus excitement," I said, patting her hand. "Is there anything I can do for you?"

Angie wagged her head. "No, thank you. I think I'd better lie down. Believe me, I'm really sorry about this, but I think I need to go home."

"I'll take you, Angie," Stan said, standing up. "You don't look good at all."

"Will you come back, Stan?" Kevin wanted to know.

He blushed. "I'll try. Sorry to have to leave your party."

"I'm the sorriest," Angie said.

"Don't worry. Just get home where it's warm and get to bed," I urged. "We'll get together again before you go back to California."

Stan helped Angie through the crowd and

outside, then Kevin turned to me. "Looks like it's just you and me now," he whispered.

"Well, uh, yes." I stared at the way Kevin had his food arranged. A napkin spread out underneath his paper plate, a little pile of mushrooms on the scalloped rim. (Obviously, he didn't like mushrooms.) Everything organized, like his music. You always got the impression he was ready for anything.

"So tell me who your piano teacher is, and how you got started." He folded his hands in front of him, and leaned forward, all ears.

"My teacher is Mrs. Putnam, on First Street. She used to play with the Cleveland Symphony. I began playing when I was little, after going to a symphony with my father," I explained. "He's a real music buff."

"Oh, yeah?" The gold flecks in Kevin's eyes stood out. "I wondered how you began. I always thought you were almost pure talent." His gaze was now a teasing one.

"Flattery will get you everywhere," I laughed, enjoying myself.

"Well, it's actually true. You sent music through my veins tonight. And when a performer can do that, he or she has power over an audience."

I knew what he was talking about. "When music moves me, I always think something mystical is happening either to me, or to the person playing it. Or, both at the same time."

"Usually both." Kevin rolled the paper

straw wrapper between his thumb and fore-finger. "And that, by the way, is a good way of putting it." He sat back, looking thoughtful, the soft light playing on his strong features. "I discovered I loved music when I was about seven. I remember thinking of it as learning a new language."

"It took me longer than most people to learn to read music," I admitted, "and I still have a tendency to play by ear."

"Did you know that some great musicians never learned to read music?" Kevin asked.

"Yes, but I think you would limit yourself by not knowing it," I said. "It would take you twice as long to learn a piece."

"That's true."

Kevin's gaze met mine, pools of warmth that made me tremble involuntarily. His eyes reflected eagerness, excitement over this common interest of ours. I couldn't remember ever talking this freely with anyone about my music.

"We have a lot in common, you and I," Kevin murmured, running a finger along the edge of his plate.

"We do," I agreed. "But I think Laurie has a lot in common with both of us, too."

"Laurie isn't into music like we are," Kevin reminded me.

"She's a singer."

"So you've told me." He was grinning.

"Well, Laurie is shy sometimes about letting people know how artistic and talented she is," I said in defense of my friend.

"Well, you talk about her too much, anyway."

"She's my best friend, and besides, I don't have that many topics of conversation."

"Baloney," Kevin laughed. "You have plenty of topics. I just bet you're a walking encyclopedia once you get going."

I laughed.

"Look, I think I ate too much," Kevin said, squashing his napkin into a ball. "I need to burn off some of this pizza in the cold. How about a walk?"

"Sounds like a good idea." It was a relief to change the subject. We rose, bundled up in our gear and strode towards the door.

"Leaving already?" Bill Wentz asked us, eyes traveling from one to the other.

"Yes. We're going to walk off our food," I informed him, and his eyebrows rose, as if to say, I'm-thinking-you-two-are-an-item.

Sometimes I get annoyed when people second-guess your situation, as I knew Bill was doing. Just because Kevin and I were together he got the impression that we were *together*-together. No one realized we were together by accident, but then I guess it didn't really matter. What people thought couldn't really hurt me.

I'd forgotten that there was a Japanese garden in back of the Rendezvous, which was absolutely beautiful in the summer.

Kevin led me over to it. "Have you seen

this in summer?" he asked, as we both surveyed the strange landscape of tiny pagodas and bridges sticking up through the snow. The little stream was frozen, and you could make out the murky flash of goldfish beneath the ice.

"Yes. It sure looks different in the winter, though. It's beautiful in an odd way."

"I think so, too," Kevin said.

The spotlights along the cobbled path cast thin beams across the snow and ice, forming alternating bars of shadow that looked eery. A wispy fog curled around our legs, and I felt as though we were walking through a set from a scary movie.

Suddenly, my feet slipped out from under me. I uttered a surprised "Oh!" as I felt myself falling.

Before I hit the ground, Kevin caught me by the elbow, quickly steadying me. "Are you all right?" he asked, not letting go of me. Instead, he wrapped his arm around my waist, until I had my footing completely. "Whew! You really scared me. You could've cracked your head on the ice."

"Thanks for rescuing me," I said, laughing from sheer relief. "I would've been in trouble, if I was alone."

In the shadowy, misty light, a flicker of a smile crossed Kevin's face before he leaned over and kissed me. His lips brushed mine gently but firmly, triggering a rush of warmth and memories mingled together, shooting through me with hot darts of recognition. I could think only of Prince Charming!

And then panic seeped in, making me remember how sweet Ricky was in the beginning. And then I thought of Laurie. "Oh, no, Laurie," I murmured, pulling abruptly away from Kevin.

I covered my face with my gloved hands. I knew Laurie didn't care as much about Kevin as I wanted her to, but I had to make him think it mattered. He stroked my hair away from my eyes.

"I know, Paula," he breathed unevenly, his deep brown eyes meeting mine. "But I've wanted to kiss you for a long time — longer than you probably imagine." His smile was mysterious.

"B-but, you're supposed to be interested in Laurie!" I exclaimed, my lips burning deliciously from his kiss. But what I didn't like, what set my heart in a panic rhythm, was the way he scattered my thoughts like so many leaves in a high wind.

"It's confusing, I know. I do like Laurie. . . ." He reached out for me, but I took a step backward, not wanting to get any closer. "But I can't help how I feel about you," he murmured softly. "How I've felt about you ever since that first night, Cinderella. Ever since I kissed you."

His gaze was steady, unrelenting, and I shivered uncontrollably. "It wasn't me you kissed, Kevin, it was Laurie. You know that!" I protested. "She's the one you went searching all over for."

"No, I think you've got it all wrong," Kevin smiled knowingly. "You're the one I went searching all over for. True, all the evidence points to Laurie — the shoe fitting her, the costume from the drama department where her mother works. All the evidence . . . except a few minor details."

"What minor details?" I challenged him, tossing my hair defiantly.

"The fact that the shoe didn't fit you, but was too big. I figured you lost it at the party because it wouldn't stay on your foot," Kevin said. And he was maddeningly correct.

"I don't want to hear anymore," I grumbled, turning my back to him, crossing my arms across my chest to keep out the cold. "It's not true."

"The other thing is the wig, which was still at your house, not Laurie's, several days after the party," he continued. I wouldn't turn around and look at him, for fear I would see him looking too pleased with himself.

"And there's more, Paula. Things you never counted on me figuring out. Like when I kissed Laurie, and I knew she wasn't Cinderella." He grasped my shoulders firmly and spun me around to face him, tipping my chin so that my gaze met his. "But when I kissed you just now, all my questions were answered."

I swallowed hard. "Not all your questions, Kevin," I answered shakily. "There are dozens of girls who wear the same size shoe as me, who could just as easily have lost a shoe like that at the party, whose feet you did not try the Cinderella slipper on." My confidence wavered, but I held my head high, determined not to let him see how upset I was.

"Oh, sure, I know. But I stopped trying the shoe on the girls at Beecher, because. . . ." He was silent a minute, gathering his thoughts for what came next. "Because I might have been able to find someone who wore the same size shoe, but I couldn't find a duplicate of those green eyes of yours."

I removed his hands from my shoulders, even though they felt nice there, and moved away from him. I didn't want to respond to that last comment, which had sent an army of goose pimples marching up and down my body. Nevertheless, whatever he chose to think, I couldn't tell him that I was Cinderella. Let him believe it, I wasn't going to admit to it.

"I just can't imagine what Laurie would think if she knew all this," I sighed heavily.

"I understand." Kevin shoved his hands in his pockets — he could tell I wanted him to keep his distance. "But what if Laurie was interested in somebody else?"

"What if? That's a hypothetical question, Kevin. She isn't, so there's nothing to discuss," I said with finality. But then I thought of Stan, and I was pretty sure he was the one Kevin was referring to. Did he know more about Laurie than she was willing to tell me?

He shrugged. "Just asking."

"You don't seem to be very loyal to Stan," I noted sarcastically. "I feel just awful about all this — even though I don't plan to ever let it happen again," I added quickly, avoiding his gaze.

"Look, Paula, I'm sorry about what happened between you and me tonight. I didn't mean to just up and kiss you. I mean. . . ." Kevin looked flustered. "I can't explain it. I'm just attracted to you, that's all. And I've had this uneasy feeling all along that Laurie wasn't Cinderella, but then I kept telling myself she had to be. Now that I've kissed you, it's clear to me who *is*."

A deep furrow appeared between his dark brown brows. "But what I can't understand is why you wanted Laurie to go out with me, after you and I had such a good time at the party. Unless, of course, Stanley is the one you really like." His look was questioning.

"Sure, I like Stan just fine, but that has nothing to do with this," I told him flatly. We were standing beneath a tree which dropped a lump of snow on my shoulder. I brushed it off and moved aside, looking into Kevin's face which appeared partly in shadow. Maybe Kevin was playing Laurie and I against each other — or trying to — as I imagined Ricky doing with Carla and me. Because maybe he got some kind of strange satisfaction out of seeing girls clamoring over him, jealous and crazy about him.

"The thing is, Kevin, *we* did not have a good time together New Year's Eve. I am *not* Cinderella," I insisted. Anger rose inside me, mixed with fear, so that I wanted to end this whole conversation, and get away from Kevin as quickly as I could. "I think you'd better take me home now."

Reluctantly, Kevin walked me to his car. As he opened the door, he asked, "We're still friends, aren't we?"

"Of course," I said stiffly, sliding onto the cold upholstery.

"I had a good time tonight," Kevin said.

"So did I," I answered. I didn't want him to think I didn't enjoy his company. Yet I couldn't have him know how much . . . and I had to keep myself from enjoying it too much.

But I also figured that we had to remain on friendly terms. After what I went through to get he and Laurie together, I didn't want to spoil it now by making things awkward.

The way I looked at it was this: Kevin and I had a short history of accidentally kissing each other. Tonight's accidental fall on the ice caused the second accidental kiss. I had just about convinced myself that I wasn't Cinderella when he confronted me with the whole thing, and I had to keep denying it, and keep him at arm's length.

Every once in awhile, as we were driving home, Kevin glanced over at me, regarding me with a puzzled look. In one way, I wished I could clear up the mystery for him, but the more he looked at me, the more tense I became, and the further back in my mind I pushed the whole Cinderella thing. All I had to do was think about what Ricky and Carla did to me, and what I was doing to Kevin came even more clearly into focus.

I didn't want Kevin attracted to me at all. I wanted to put out that fire in his eyes — and the one in my own heart — before it got dangerous.

Ten

Meg glanced up from her overflowing bowl of Cheerios to ask me, "Where are you going this early in the morning?"

"Ice skating," I answered. Laurie and I weren't often up before ten on Sundays.

"I'd like to come. I don't have anything to do today," Meg mentioned as offhandedly as a ten-year-old knows how.

Those big blue eyes were quite convincing, however. And I hadn't taken her anywhere in a long time. Meg is a good skater, like Reggie. Not like me. I have the worst sense of balance on record. I think that's the real reason why, ever since I learned how to ride a bicycle, I vowed never to become an athlete. Piano playing doesn't require much balance, only enough to hold yourself on a stool.

"Okay, Meg. Hurry up and get ready," I told her.

"Yahoo!" Meg whooped, nearly upsetting

her bowl. She got up, ran to her room, and the next thing I heard was junk being tossed around as she searched in her closet for her skates.

Meg's bedroom looks like mine used to, before Ricky Castle and I broke up. Of course, I'm still not totally organized, but after Ricky scattered my emotions, I had to put some order into my life, so I cleaned my bedroom from top to bottom. I started hanging up my clothes after I wore them. I vacuumed once a week. There were no more candy wrappers and cookie crumbs or rumpled tissues spilling out of the wastebasket. No more sheet music covering my desk top. Instead, it sat in a neat pile, where I could page through it easily. I bought posters, framed them myself, and hung them up on the walls. All these things made me feel good about myself — something Ricky did *not* do.

The thought of Ricky made me shudder. So much had happened since then, but the experience of loving him had changed me, and would probably always be with me. And after last night, I was worried about Kevin, and making sure nothing hurt my friendship with Laurie — like what happened with Carla.

Meg appeared with her skates slung over one shoulder. "Ready!" she called.

I followed her into the hall when Laurie rang the doorbell. Meg answered it. "I'm going, too," she beamed.

"Oh, yeah, Squirt? I see you did some fancy

talking." Laurie ruffled her hair playfully.

We piled into Laurie's car, turned the radio up loud, and sped along, singing. Laurie's resonant, alto voice kept the rest of us on key, leading us through each tune. When we reached the park and set Meg loose on the ice, she spied a couple of friends and took off after them, leaving us free to talk.

"So how'd it go after you left the school?" Laurie asked.

"Stanley had to take his cousin Angie home early because she didn't feel well. Too much pizza and jet lag," I explained, shoving a foot into a skate.

"Oh, really? So what did you and Kevin do?" Interest perked in her voice.

Immediately, I felt guilty, remembering how his lips felt on mine. "We ate dinner, walked around, talked about you, and he brought me home." A wave of guilt crashed over me, but Laurie didn't notice anything amiss.

We moved onto the ice. "You've been different since you've been seeing Kevin," I said, watching Laurie's eager expression: the parted lips, the brightness in her round blue eyes.

"I hadn't noticed any change," she replied absently. "I think he's very nice, and I like doubling with you and Stan most of all."

A mysterious smile tugged at the corners of her mouth as we skated. She can be so secretive at times, and I know how to read her like a book — except when she does this.

Laurie skated a little ahead of me, because I'm a timid skater, and it's about all I can do to keep out of everyone's way and not fall down. Meg and Laurie had fun pirouetting and jumping on the ice, and I was content to watch them and applaud.

When we were sufficiently frozen and hungry, Laurie invited us to her house for lunch. "Mom went shopping yesterday and we've got tons of food."

We left the rink and headed for Laurie's house, where she fixed sandwiches, soup, and cocoa.

"Skating really builds up an appetite," I said, when I was finished devouring two peanut butter sandwiches and a bowl of soup. "I've got a science report to finish, so I'd better get home."

"Why don't you spend the night here?" Laurie urged. "We can do our homework together."

"It's a school night," I protested, knowing Mom would say the same thing when I asked her.

"We'll go to bed early," Laurie said, grinning mischievously. Laurie is a great one for telling scary stories which make it impossible to fall asleep, especially with an imagination like mine replaying horrible things in living color.

"Well, let's take Meg home and see if it's all right. Mom might just be grateful that she's had the house to herself today, and be in a great mood."

As it turned out, our mother was busy sewing at five o'clock when we marched in. And she *was* happy to have had the day to herself. She said yes to our request, just making me promise to get to bed early at Laurie's.

When we got back to Laurie's, we studied, ate dinner, and I wrote my report on mollusks with the help of the encyclopedia and a marine biology text my dad lent me. Later I crawled into the extra twin bed in Laurie's room, ready for her onslaught of hair-raising tales.

Instead, she began with, "You and Stan make the perfect couple."

I nearly choked. "Stan's nice, Laurie, but not what I really want. I mean, I guess all I want is fun, so it's okay." I changed the subject. "Did you ever kiss Kevin, Laurie?"

"No, not really *kiss* him. He's kissed me briefly on the cheek, the hello and good-bye kind of kisses, but nothing serious."

"Do you think it's possible to tell one person's kiss from another's?" I pondered aloud.

She burst out laughing. "Paula, since when did you get so dense? Honestly, you must know some people turn you on, and some people don't."

"But do you think you could tell the difference between Kevin's kiss and someone else's if you were blindfolded?" I persisted.

"It would depend on who the 'someone else' was," she explained. "But I'm sure I could tell. When Don kissed me, it was exciting. Sometimes I felt fireworks just from being close to him. He didn't even have to touch me, but when he did, sparks flew."

"Oh, yeah?" I blinked in the darkness, suddenly knowing exactly what Laurie was talking about. "What do you call that reaction?"

"It's chemistry, Paula," Laurie sighed. "It isn't often you find the right chemistry."

"Hmmm." I watched her readjust her pillows, and switch off the light. "Laurie, if I found it, would I know it right away?"

Laurie giggled. "Paula, are you serious? Of course, you would know it. You knew with Ricky, didn't you?"

"Uh huh," I replied distantly. I knew Laurie was right, but I also knew these feelings weren't necessarily lasting. Ricky certainly didn't have the same effect on me that he used to.

"But do you think you can develop chemistry, where you didn't think there was any?" I persisted.

Laurie propped herself on one elbow and stared at me in the dark.

"I suppose."

"Like, for instance, could you do something to convince Kevin that you're really Cinderella — more than we already have. Create sparks, maybe."

"You can't create sparks out of thin air," she muttered. "On that note, Paula, I'm saying good-night."

"Good-night." I lay awake for a long time, thinking of how Laurie could attract Kevin in a way that he would never look at me again. But what kept interrupting my thoughts was the memory of Kevin's kiss, the taste of his lips, and the way his touch sent little shivers all through me. I was afraid of him, afraid of how I now felt, afraid of what kind of a guy Kevin was. I wished that he had never kissed me.

I was just drifting off to sleep when I heard Laurie's muffled voice rise from her pillow. "Oh, Stan," she whispered, so unmistakably, it took my breath away.

Eleven

At school Monday, I kept thinking of Laurie whispering Stan's name in the night. It wasn't my imagination. I was sure of that. And after much thought, I knew I had to say something to her about it. If Laurie was in love with Stan and not telling me because she figured *I* was interested in him and didn't want to upset what she thought was our relationship, then she had to know how I really felt about Stanley.

Midmorning, I happened to come to my locker because I forgot something, and saw Stan across the hall from Laurie. She was pulling her gym clothes from our locker. I watched them from the staircase landing. He stared at her, and she stared back, a wistful, dreamy expression on her face that I hadn't seen her wear since Don left. The flush of her cheeks, the shine in her eyes told me the whole story — Laurie was crazy about Stan.

Certainly, it proved to me beyond any doubt that Laurie's night whisperings were very real. What she felt and dreamed about, she had to keep secret from me.

I decided to go to class without the book I needed, just so that I didn't have to interrupt this scene for Laurie. Everything started to fall into place in my mind. Like how Stan behaved toward Laurie, for instance. How the two of them had struck up an easy conversation the night the four of us had gone to the club. And how Laurie had been so interested in that hockey game. Then, I recalled Laurie's behavior lately, thinking it was because she was in love with Kevin. But it had nothing to do with Kevin — because when we double-dated, she was able to see Stan. And that was why she had stars in her eyes.

I remembered catching Stan staring at Laurie on several occasions, and the more I thought about it, the more I could picture the two of them together.

I thought about this all during my next class, but had to put it aside at lunch because I was deluged by students congratulating me on my performance.

"Paula, you were fantastic," Terri Struthers exclaimed.

"Still can't get over you," Dale Bench said, buttonholing me at the snack bar. He's on the newspaper staff. "Do you have time for an interview this lunch period?"

"Interview? Me? Oh, sure," I beamed.

"Good. Stay here. Just let me get some food."

Dale and I trooped down to the newspaper room, which is about the messiest classroom in the entire school. It's actually a big basement, and every wall is covered by some kind of article or photograph depicting a fascinating piece of news. There are copies of the *Sun Times* strewn all over the long tables, ready to be stacked and folded for distribution.

"Is this the first time you've ever received wide acclaim for your talent?" Dale asked me.

"No. I've done lots of recitals. Once I was paid a basket of apples and five dollars for playing for a Women's Club luncheon."

Dale laughed. He had a crooked nose, wide mouth, and light blue eyes. "Didn't you used to go out with Ricky Castle?"

I stiffened. "Yes, but you're not going to put that in the paper, are you?"

He shrugged. "It is a human interest piece, Paula."

"But that's not a very interesting thing about me. I can tell you others. Delete Ricky, please."

"Okay," he said, grinning. "What's your favorite breakfast cereal?"

"Grape-nuts. Boy, this is beginning to sound like *People* magazine."

"We do our best." Dale flipped to a fresh page. "How much do you practice?"

"At least two hours a day, sometimes more."

"Do you play other music, besides classical? And what you do in orchestra?"

"Yes. I enjoy blues and popular music. Why limit myself, I figure."

"Favorite musicians?"

"Peter Serkin, in the way of classical pianists, and also Elton John and Stevie Wonder," I replied.

"The most important influences in your life?"

"Probably my parents, and my piano teacher, Mrs. Putnam."

Dale began gathering up his stuff. "The bell's ready to ring, Paula. Thanks for your time. This'll be a pretty good article."

"Am I interesting enough?"

"Oh, yeah. I can see the headlines now: 'Catch a Rising Star — Paula Rizzoni,'" he said.

"That's a great headline." I couldn't stop smiling. "I love it."

"Thought you would. Thanks, Paula. I'll see you around."

My next class was orchestra. Kevin came over and said hi. His arm brushed against mine, sending a thrill through me, which I tried to ignore. Why did he have to have this effect on me?

"Everyone's raving about you," he said, smiling.

There was something behind the soft

brown eyes that made me shiver — a hesitation, a waiting.

"I know. But they're talking about you, too," I told him.

"Popular, aren't you?"

I blushed. Fortunately, the bell rang. But for the rest of the period, my hands perspired so heavily that they slid off the piano keys. Mr. McEllis's eagle eye zeroed in on me every so often, and I knew he was thinking that my success had gone to my head, and now I couldn't handle it. But what I couldn't handle more was Kevin Stevens standing close to me, playing the flute.

I tried to keep my eyes on his fingers, which fluttered over the keys — not looking at his mouth, or his face, which wore the rapt expression of someone totally immersed in the music. I also tried to keep the notes in my head — dancing, lilting notes that pushed into the room, taking over with their power.

When class was dismissed, I rushed out of the room before Kevin could think of approaching me. I was too nervous to speak to him. What I desperately needed was to talk to Laurie, and unravel this whole mess.

I finally found her after school at our locker.

"Where've you been all day?" she quizzed me.

"I was being interviewed by Dale Bench at lunch," I told her.

"My, aren't we the celeb!" she said, smiling at me. "How're things with Stanley?" she asked after a moment.

"Oh, uh, fine," I mumbled. "Laurie, I have to talk to you."

"Well, shoot." She was distracted, trying to dislodge a book stuck in the back of the locker. This was hardly the time to talk about this, but I was filled to bursting.

I took a deep breath. "I know you don't want me to know this, but I can't help but see it."

"Paula, what're you talking about?" She stared at me as though I was crazed. "You've been so weird lately."

"I know you're crazy over Stanley." There, it was out in the open.

"What? How do you know that?" she demanded, yanking the book from the locker.

"It's written all over your face — might as well be lit up in neon."

She laughed. "No kidding? Well, I'm *not* crazy about Stanley."

"Don't worry, Laurie," I tried to assure her. "I'm very happy. He doesn't mean anything to me — never has. Remember us talking about chemistry last night? Well, he and I don't have it. But I know he likes you."

"That's crazy, Paula," she retorted, clearly ruffled. "So what makes you think that I like him?"

"You talked in your sleep last night. You said, 'Oh, Stan' in this soft voice. . . ."

"Come off it." She frowned, twirling a reddish-gold lock behind her ear.

"Honest, you did."

She sighed. "Oh, all right, so I did. What does it mean? Now you're an interpreter of dreams?"

"No, silly. It means that you should let Stan know that you're interested in him. I saw you two together at your locker between classes, and if that wasn't love, I need my eyes checked."

"I think it's just a strong attraction right now," Laurie admitted. "Are you sure about this — him meaning nothing to you?"

"Yes, I told you he means nothing to me. You two should be together." I leaned against the other lockers and watched her. "You know, last night when we were talking about chemistry, I was thinking about how nice it would be if you could create a chemistry between you and Kevin. But then you said that wouldn't work, and I laid awake a long time wondering why not? Why couldn't you just throw two people together and have them eventually stir up some kind of sparks?

"But then I got to thinking about Stanley Kolby and I, and how, no matter how nice a guy he is, there'll never be any sparks between us. I don't have a whole lot to talk about with him. I tried to imagine creating sparks with him, and I couldn't come up with a place to begin." I sighed.

"And that works perfectly for me, not having any sparks, since I'm afraid of them, anyway," I said sagely.

Laurie shook her head, shoving her books

in her bookbag. "Oh, Paula, what're we going to do about this mess? I'm supposed to go out with Kevin this weekend, and I think Stan's supposed to invite you out, too. You know, I was happy when you started going out with Stanley, because I figured I'd get to see him on our double dates, and also, if he didn't fall for you, maybe he'd get up enough nerve to ask me out. There was always this . . ." — she flapped her hand in the air, searching for a word — ". . . crazy feeling between us, but neither of us ever said or did anything before. I mean, we had a couple of classes together, but you know how that goes.

"But with Kevin," she went on, "I get another feeling, a lack of magic. We often have trouble talking. In fact a lot of our conversations are about you. It's you he wants to be with. D'ya know, we never kiss now, and I'm just as relieved that we don't, because I keep thinking that he'd rather be kissing you!"

"I don't want to kiss him!" I declared hotly.

"Look what happens when we're all out together," she noted. "You end up talking to Kevin and I talk to Stan."

I groaned. "You know how I feel about Kevin. I'm not looking for a trade, if that's what you're thinking. But what're we going to do? Should I turn down a date with Stan if he asks me out?" Then I thought for a moment, and answered my own question. "Well, come to think of it, my invitations from Stan don't come direct, anyway."

Laurie stuck out her lower lip in a thoughtful pose.

"Let's just see what happens. Play it by ear, so to speak," she decided.

"Sounds weird," I said.

"Trust me," she said. "I've got rehearsals now. See ya later." She clutched her books to her chest and scooted down the hall. I marveled at how she had just spit out all her feelings about Stan when I confronted her, and how loyal she was to me: how she wouldn't have gone out with Stanley if she thought it would hurt me, and she would've held her attraction to him in check because of me. If he had liked me instead of her, then she never would've said a word.

And I guessed Stan was the same kind of guy. A real prince — pardon the expression. I wasn't sure the same could be said of someone like Kevin.

For just the thought of Kevin left a light fear fluttering against my rib cage.

Twelve

The week moved along very quickly. Laurie was busy with rehearsals nearly every night after school, and I spent my time practicing for a piano recital. I noticed Stan pass our locker during the times Laurie visited it. Otherwise, I hardly ever saw Stan during the day, and when we did run into each other, he only said hello, not much more. And no mention of a date for Friday night.

I knew Kevin had invited Laurie out, but she wasn't sure what she would do about it, yet. Could she stop seeing Kevin and go out with Stanley? I knew Kevin was attracted to me last weekend, but I wondered if that was on isolated incident. Another accident.

Still, I could not ignore the fact that every time Kevin looked at me in orchestra, something happened to me. Something came undone inside me. I lost my place in the music, and I had to look away. Often, I stared at the

American flag whipping in the wind outside the music building. Anything but face those intense eyes that threatened to tug me into a vortex of emotion that I wasn't sure I could swim out of.

Outside the music room things were not much better for me. At home, while closing my eyes during a very moving passage in the piece I was playing, Kevin's face appeared before me, smiling. It reminded me of how totally absorbed I once was with Ricky. I had even been distracted from my playing. Ricky, with all the pangs of hurt and pain gone, still governed my feelings toward Kevin. I guess I just didn't like the idea that a boy could dissolve my concentration that way.

One day after orchestra, Kevin walked out of class with cute Danielle Corley. I strode ahead of him, casting a breezy smile his way as I passed. Jealousy curled around my heart. I wished it didn't bother me to see him with other girls — other than Laurie. But maybe it was better that Laurie didn't date him. Maybe she was better off with someone reliable like Stanley.

Funny, just that morning, Laurie announced her intention of inviting Stan to eat lunch with her.

"I'm sick of all this intrigue," she exclaimed in exasperation. "Stan is too shy to make a move and I don't see any other way to break the ice."

I grinned. "It ought to melt pretty easily."

All this was spiraling around in my mind, so that I didn't hear Kevin run up behind me.

"Paula!" he shouted.

I turned.

"Got a date for lunch?"

"No, why?"

"You look like you're in a hurry to meet someone," he said, cocking his head to one side.

"I usually have lunch with Laurie, but she's having lunch with Stan today," I blurted out, realizing almost immediately what I'd just said. *Oh, no, did I spill the beans, or what? What would Laurie do when she found out I said this?* "I mean, I think they're working on a report together."

"Oh, yeah? Laurie never mentioned it." Kevin studied me. My skin rippled under his scrutiny. "I can picture them together, somehow. Can you?"

"Well, I never thought about it," I said nervously.

"I'm free for lunch, in case you're interested," he said with a grin that lit up his eyes.

My heart was in my throat. I had planned to use the lunch hour as a study period at the library. Or I could find Sandy Martin, a friend and good person to talk to. But lunch with Kevin? I giggled, a nervous reaction, I'm sure. I couldn't exactly turn him down very gracefully. Laurie had left me wide open for this, by asking Stan to lunch.

"Did you bring or do you buy?" I asked.

"Buy." We walked together to the snack bar, discussing orchestra. Kevin turned to me. "You've been running out of orchestra early this week."

"I've been very busy," I said, not wanting him to know that I did it because of him, that I was really afraid of the way he made me feel.

"That explains it," was all he said. We bought sandwiches, then went into the auditorium to eat. A few heads turned when we entered, and I wondered briefly how long it would take for news of our lunch together to travel through the entire student body.

"Okay, tell me what's going on with Laurie and Stan," Kevin said, taking a bite of his tuna fish sandwich.

That seemed like a safe enough subject. I breathed a small sigh of relief. "I only know Laurie invited Stan to lunch," I said.

"Yes, but why?" A mischievous glint danced in his eyes. "And what do we all do about dating this weekend if those two end up together? Any ideas?"

I shrugged, but I could feel the heat climbing into my cheeks. "Well, Stan hasn't asked me out, yet, but that's not out of character for him. Usually he asks you or Laurie to ask me."

Kevin grinned. "True. This makes life easier for you and me, in a way. Maybe you'd like to go to a movie with me, instead." He posed it as a statement, and when his hand covered mine and sent goose bumps racing up my arm, I eased mine away. I didn't want him to be offended. "I really like your company, Paula. I'm not just asking you because this happened with Stan and Laurie."

Kevin's gaze roamed over my face. I felt his eyes studying everything about me, making me self-conscious. "Well, you did say you wanted Stan to have a social life," I mumbled.

"You didn't answer my question," he said matter-of-factly.

"I didn't know you asked one." I evaded him, but I didn't think, by the intense look he shot at me, that he was amused.

"I'm trying to ask you out."

"I-I'm sorry," I stuttered, wiping my mouth with a paper napkin. All of a sudden, the sandwich I was eating formed a leaden lump in my throat, and I felt sick. I wanted to bolt out of my seat and get away . . . fast, but instead, I sat rooted to my seat. "You're a nice guy, but —"

"I think we already know we like each other," Kevin said gently.

A thrill ran through me as I recalled the firm brush of his lips, the way his arms encircled my waist, the way it felt to dance with him.

"I don't know how I feel about you, Kevin," I replied shakily. "But I'm busy all this weekend, so I can't go out with you."

His eyebrows rose in twin arches as he stood up, squishing his sandwich wrapper and backhanding it into the garbage can. "Okay, fair enough. I didn't know you had such a full schedule, but maybe some other time." I could tell by his eyes, that he was disappointed. My heart turned. "Well, thanks for having lunch with me. It was fun." He grinned.

"You're welcome," I told him, but I wanted to say that it was fun for me, too, because when he walked away, he left me feeling a little empty, and a little hungry inside.

"So, from what Stan told me — shyly, of course —" Laurie explained to Meg and I while flipping through her closet, "I gather that Kevin came to him and told him that it was okay if Stan asked me out. He understood how Stan felt and he could see how happy we look together. Of course, I can just imagine poor Stanley blushing ten shades of red at that, can't you?"

She twirled in front of us, holding a soft pink lambswool sweater up to herself. Her eyes shone bright with emotion, her cheeks flushed prettily.

"That's the perfect sweater, Laurie, with your wine-red pants," I said.

"Yeah, okay, but I wondered, do Stan and I look happy together, or is it my imagination?"

I rolled my eyes as she slipped on the red pants. They fit perfectly; obviously she hadn't grown or gained weight since last winter. "Yes, you do look happy together. I noticed that even before I knew what I was looking for," I reassured her.

"Stanley also said that Kevin asked you out, but you turned him down." Laurie was now talking a little absently, as if her mind was still caught on Stanley, even though she was capable of talking about other subjects.

"That's right." I was winding a ball of yarn that Crispy, Laurie's calico kitten, had strewn across the floor.

"Why don't you want to go out with him?" Laurie asked.

"You know why," I said, my voice betraying my misery.

But as I said it, I realized I hardly knew why myself anymore. Just in the last few days, I felt like I'd been on a roller coaster of feelings. Whenever I saw Kevin, I would have to look away, concentrate on something else, pushing all thoughts of him out of my mind. When Laurie and Kevin had talked about her going out with Stan and canceling their weekend date, I suddenly felt very vulnerable. And when we were sitting in orchestra and Kevin's gaze would meet mine, I'd read the question in his eyes, which I couldn't answer: "Why won't you go out with me?"

How could I tell him it was because of Ricky, because he reminded me so much of a boy who had hurt me so much, that I could never feel comfortable with him? How could he know that I'd vowed never to fall for anyone like that again, and that's why I had to turn him down?

That night, while Laurie was out on her first real date with Stan Kolby, I took my little sister to the movies. We chose a remake of Tarzan, which was not my first choice, but afterward I was glad we saw it because it wasn't romantic and it was stupidly funny. When I'm not exactly happy, I like to be distracted by laughter. I'm convinced that laughter is a really good medicine for just about any problem. It doesn't solve problems, naturally, but it does take the edge off them, and gives you a new perspective. I'm always pleased when I can forget my troubles for just an hour or so, with some funny movie or book.

Anyway, Meg liked it and talked about it constantly, all the way to The Soda Shop afterwards.

"I liked the part where he began acting like an ape and started swinging from the chandeliers," Meg said.

There was a funny knocking sound coming from the front of the car. I wondered how long it had been since my father had had the car tuned up, because he was usually pretty good about that kind of thing. Yet lately, he had a lot on his mind.

When we turned into a parking space at The Soda Shop, the noise went away, and I hoped it wouldn't return once we started home again. I made a mental note to tell Dad about it when we got home.

We ordered strawberry milkshakes and burgers.

"I'll bet you wish you were here with Kevin," Meg said, watching me for a reaction over the rim of her tall, tulip-shaped glass.

"I'll bet I don't," I said, waving at Colette Stuart and Sarah Duncan, who were walking toward us.

Colette smiled at me warmly. "Paula, how're you doing? This is your little sister, Meg?"

"Yes, that's me."

"Where's Stan tonight? And Kevin and Laurie?" she quizzed me. Honestly, if a trap door had presented itself for me to fall through, I would've welcomed it. Usually I like Colette a lot, but at that moment I was not crazy about her.

"Well, uh, we're not out together, as you can see. The Fantastic Foursome has split up," I announced, shrugging. I figured the news was going to hit the grapevine soon enough anyway, so what was I all embarrassed about?

Then Meg had to get into the act. "Laurie's out with Stan tonight, instead of Kevin," she replied. "And Paula was going to —"

Suddenly, her expression crumpled as my foot met her shin under the table. "Paula was going to a movie with me," she finished, but we both knew that wasn't what she intended to say originally.

I smiled blandly at Colette, who looked thoroughly confused.

"Don't worry about it, Colette," I assured her. "Laurie and Stan will probably be in later and you can ask them all about it." Then I turned to Meg. "We'd better go. See you, Colette."

"See ya," she blinked in complete bewilderment as we strode out of The Soda Shop.

Once outside, Meg exploded in giggles. "She sure looked funny when you told her about the four of you," she said, but I was focusing on the green VW bug in the parking area.

Kevin's car. Not wanting him to notice me, I hustled Meg into the car and drove out onto the open road. What a relief — and she didn't even see him, which was better. I didn't want to have to explain any more to Meg tonight.

But suddenly, the car started acting up, making all kinds of clunking noises. We were on a deserted, tree-lined stretch of road, about five miles from our house.

"What is it?" Meg cried, peering out into the black night. Behind us, car headlights shone a silver wand over our car as I eased over to the side of the road. The car behind us pulled over, too.

I started to open the door, when a figure blocked my way.

"Need some help, lady?" a familiar voice

asked, and then, even in the dark, I recognized that grin. *Kevin*.

I let out a sigh of relief. "Oh, how did you know?"

"I saw you leave the parking lot, so I followed you, on the off chance you might talk to me," he said, opening the door wide. "Let's take a look under the hood and see what the trouble is."

Armed with a flashlight and a greasy rag, Kevin looked under the hood, poking and pulling at various things which I didn't know the names of. Cars were never my strong suit.

"Well, it looks like you have a busted fan belt," he said finally, pulling up a limp donut-shaped object and holding it to the light.

"What does this mean?" I asked him, as if he were the doctor.

"It means that you should probably leave the car here tonight, and come get it tomorrow." His cinnamon-brown eyes met mine. "And I could give you a ride home right now."

I hesitated for a moment.

"Well, uh, that'd be very nice," I said, a tremor creeping into my voice. After all, I was totally helpless: here, on a dark road, with my kid sister and a broken fan belt. Hesitation gave way to pure need.

Kevin helped Meg into the back seat of his VW. Then I slid into the front seat beside him.

Something happened to my resolve that

night. I felt it slipping, and all because Kevin appeared out of the dark night to rescue us. He came and scooped us up into his warm little car, and deposited Meg and me safely at our door. I wondered for a moment if he had followed me because he wanted to ask me out again, but it didn't really matter. What mattered was that Kevin was there when I needed him.

"You saved our lives," Meg declared dramatically, as she got of the car when we reached home.

"I don't know what we would've done without you," I told Kevin appreciatively. He covered my hands with his, and squeezed them. Tingles shot up my arm.

Then he smiled. "Glad I could help you," he replied. I started to leave, but he tugged me back. "Do you think maybe now you might go out with me?"

I laughed. "Call me," I said softly. I didn't know what my answer was going to be — but as I watched him drive away, I had a pretty good idea.

Thirteen

Kevin did call me and invited me out for Saturday night. We planned to go to a movie. He arrived at my house right on time, which was just before my parents were due to go out. Of course, they asked the usual round of parent questions, and Dad asked Kevin about his group.

"Sorry my father gave you the third degree," I told him on the way out to the car.

"No big deal. They're your basic parents, aren't they?" he laughed and took my hand. Then he lowered his voice. "And you're your basic Cinderella."

My breath caught sharply. He knows! I thought in panic. I decided the best thing to do was pretend I didn't know what he was talking about.

We got in the car. Kevin leaned over to pick a piece of thread out of my hair, turning the inside light on to see better. Then he tugged on a strand, pulling me towards him, my mouth towards his. We kissed for a long moment.

"I've been wanting to do that since I first saw you tonight." He stroked my cheek.

"Nobody would've guessed," I teased him, and he kissed me again.

Snow flurried in big, papery flakes as we drove along the tree-lined route toward town. The windshield wipers kept up a steady rhythm with the song on the radio, which Kevin hummed. We were sitting close together and his voice reverberated along my skin, making me shiver.

"I can turn up the heater," he offered.

"No, thanks. It's warm in here."

He laid his hand over mine. "We must keep these piano fingers warm," he said.

"What about your mouth?" I said softly, looking into his eyes.

He pulled over to the side of the road, and put his hands on my shoulders. "We place it on yours — to keep it warm," he whispered, kissing me deeply.

My mind formed his name, as his kiss took hold of me, making me weak. Then he let go of me and drove back onto the road, heading toward the theater.

When we got to the parking lot, Kevin turned to me and patted my hand. "How do you feel about me now, Paula?"

I was afraid my actions were speaking louder than words at that time. I guessed I could act like I could take him or leave him, but I think Kevin knew better. The way I accepted his kiss spoke for itself, and the way I felt when I looked at him must be obvious. But I didn't like feeling so vulnerable, so painfully scared of being hurt.

"I like you, Kevin," I said softly, opening the car door, in the hopes of ending this conversation.

He leaned over, closed the door and kissed me again. "I wanted to hear you say it," he said. "Now, let's go to the movies."

I usually consider a movie an ordinary date, but there was nothing ordinary about being with Kevin. He was interested in everything — the art deco architecture, where the movie was filmed, what the lead stars were doing at the moment. I found myself interested in the way the beam of light from the projector played across Kevin's features.

I would remember this moment forever: the smell of popcorn, the rusty whir of the projector, the feel of Kevin's arm around me. It was hard to concentrate on the movie because those impressions were so strong.

The jist of the story was a woman falling in love with her doctor. He doesn't know she's in love with him, and she is going through every imaginable contortion to show her feelings, without being obvious. (Of course, she was obvious to everyone in the audience!)

So, to make a long story short, she leaves a letter in his examining room expressing how she feels, and he comes to her, and of course, they get together.

During the last kissing scene, Kevin squeezed my hand, and whispered in my ear, "Are they like us?"

"Not quite," I giggled, for his breath tickled my ears. "You're not a doctor, remember?"

"And you don't leave me little notes." He smiled in the darkness.

Little did he know that I had to hold my feelings in by the reins — yank them down to a mild gallop.

When the movie was over, Kevin suggested dancing. "And the best place I know is the rec room at my house. I have a great collection of records and tapes." He laced his arm through mine. "Come on. I want Mom and Dad to meet you, anyway, Paula."

We climbed in the car and sped over to Kevin's. In the dark, the white house stood out against the stark winter landscape, strangely defiant of its surroundings. The house was about a hundred years old, two-stories, and surrounded by sloping, tree-studded grounds. I followed Kevin up the slippery side path.

Kevin's parents were watching television in the living room, when we walked in. Mr. Stevens was a squarely built man with short-cropped brown hair. It was obvious that Kevin had inherited his father's features.

"Nice to meet you," Mr. Stevens and I said together.

"Nice to see you again, Paula," Kevin's mother chimed in. "How's the music going?"

"I'm practicing for my class recital which is coming up soon," I explained.

"What're you playing?" Mr. Stevens wanted to know.

"The piano — Moonlight Sonata."

"Difficult piece."

I glanced at Kevin. His eyebrows rose in twin arches of surprise — I'd never mentioned the piece to him. "We'll be downstairs if you need us," he told his parents, and we parted.

The rec room had obviously gone through the changes of kids growing up, complete with watercolors and fingerpaints on the walls, sports trophies and plaques, which I wanted to look at more closely. But Kevin took me in his arms, and I forgot about them.

We danced to some slow, popular songs. Kevin's embrace moved me beyond words or feelings. Only music gave me a sensation like this before, and now this was sweeter — more insistent, and perhaps more painful because I didn't want it to end.

It was another moment I would always remember: feeling Kevin's breath warm against my cheek, his arms tight on my waist, our gentle swaying.

Then Kevin smiled down at me. "You know, this is another clue, Paula. If I could've held you in my arms when I tried on that shoe, I would've known instantly that you were Cinderella. Nobody feels as nice to hold as you."

"People would think you were crazy if they heard you say that," I said, burying my face in the hollow of his shoulder.

"No crazier than if you told them you'd found Prince Charming," he said, ruffling my hair with his words.

I didn't think about it until much later — that I'd forgotten to insist that I wasn't Cinderella. It would have been hopeless, anyway, because even if a word hadn't been spoken about it, Kevin would've known by now, without a doubt.

Fourteen

Kevin invited me to watch him play at The Cellar on Saturday night. The minute I walked in the door, I loved everything about the place, from the old fashioned posters tacked on the walls to the ginger cat asleep on the worn rag rug in front of the stone fireplace.

Kevin suggested I play the piano while the band tuned up, and he got our refreshments. It was exciting to sit at the piano onstage, striking chords for Gus and Roy. When Kevin returned, he snuck up behind me, and put his arms on my shoulders, while I played.

"You are wonderful, Paula," he whispered into my ear.

"Oh, Kevin, how do you expect me to play with you here?" I asked teasingly.

"I don't," he said as he sat down next to

me and lifted my hand from the keys. "It's time for me to go on."

We laughed, he kissed me, and I stepped down from the stage. Kevin had reserved a special seat for me in front. As I glanced around the room, I recognized familiar faces from school, including a group of girls who sat down near me, drooling over Kevin.

Kevin smiled at them when they started clapping, and I felt my jealousy rising up again. Why did he have to pay attention to them at all? They were so obvious.

Alison Berendt, from Edwards High School, flipped her silky ponytail over her shoulder and blew Kevin a kiss. He closed his eyes and blew into his flute, sending notes soaring through the room. He played two of his own creations that I'd heard him do in orchestra, and then he made an announcement.

"I'm dedicating this song to two friends of mine. You've probably heard it before."

He launched into the song, which he played on the saxophone. The deep, resonant tones dropped into the silence, causing goose bumps to creep along my skin. I made a note to ask him which two friends the song was written for.

Kevin was on his way down to meet me when Alison Berendt buttonholed him. Since I was so close, I could hear every word she said:

"Do you think you could show me some

things on the flute sometime?" she asked in her little-girl voice. "I'm a good player, but you have some interesting techniques I'd like to learn."

Interesting techniques. What a line! A burning began in my heart and traveled all the way to my throat.

"Well, uh, give me a call sometime, Alison," Kevin mumbled, glancing over at me.

"Maybe we can meet somewhere, and talk," she persisted.

"Sure. Let's talk about it later. I don't have a very long break," he told her.

Whew! That was lucky. But Alison wasn't the only one giving Kevin the eye. Looking at his watch, then at me, he shook his head.

"Sorry, Paula, I'm out of time. We'll talk after the show."

And with that, he was back on stage. His hair glistened under the lights, and the way he moved made me tingle all over. His eyes met mine, and I felt warm beneath his scrutiny. Everything felt all right again, but I was thinking that it would be nice to have him all to myself, not have to share him with these girls. . . .

And then I saw Carla. She was alone, which was unusual, but she smiled uncertainly at me. I managed a smile — until she lifted her glass of Coke, and I saw the ring. It was the same ring Ricky once gave me, the one I gave back to him when we split up: a class ring, too big for my finger, that I had to put tape and nail polish on to make it fit. I smiled bitterly, recalling what it was like to wear it, and to pull it off my finger and hand it to him.

I turned away and looked back at Kevin. Me, Paula Rizzoni, the girl who was never going to fall in love again, especially not with someone as attractive and charismatic as Kevin, had done it. I was a hopeless case, and I wasn't sure I liked being this vulnerable.

After the show, Alison glided over to Kevin with her phone number. I don't think she knew he and I were together, or if she did, she obviously didn't care very much. He was a free spirit, anyway, wasn't he? We weren't really going together. We were just friends.

Other girls flocked around Kevin after Alison left. I finished my Coke and just sat there, not knowing quite what to do, while I listened to an unending stream of praise:

"Oooh, you were fabulous."

"When will you play here again?"

"I loved the songs you wrote yourself."

I thought I was going to be *sick*.

"Paula, are you ready to go?" Kevin stood over me, casting a shadow over the table.

"Yes," I said, then added, "if you're finished with your fans."

On the way out to the car, I told Kevin he was really great. "But everyone's already told you that."

"Your professional opinion means more

to me, Paula." He squeezed my hand.

"The others looked like pretty attractive opinions to me," I said sarcastically.

He shrugged. "Not really."

I stopped in my tracks, jerking him to a halt. "What do you mean? Alison Berendt was all over you."

He arched an eyebrow. "She's interested in music. Big deal."

"It could be," I grumbled.

Kevin reached for my shoulders. "What do you mean by that, Paula?"

I had no right to carry on like this. We didn't know each other all that well to be making these kinds of demands. Why was I so upset? I couldn't stop myself, though. "Usually when girls are that enthusiastic over a guy, it means they're pretty interested in him," I tried to explain.

"Not necessarily."

"You'd have to be blind not to notice it," I kept up, as we walked out to his car.

Kevin slid behind the wheel of the car, and suddenly pounded his fist on the dashboard. "Does it matter if they are? I'm not interested in *them*," he responded defensively.

"It must go to your head, though."

"It doesn't," Kevin insisted. "Why do you think it has to?"

"Because of my experience," I told him flatly.

"With Ricky Castle? Are you comparing *me* to *him*?"

I was so tense, I could feel my heart pounding in my ears, but nothing else. "My experience with popular, good-looking guys is that you always have to worry about them being lured away. They give you a lot of heartaches."

"Really?" Kevin uttered a hollow laugh.

"Yeah. I just feel like I can't get into anything like that again. It's too scary for me." In my mind, I sounded so logical.

Kevin leaned over and stroked my hair. I was trembling then. "Look, Paula. I'm not your ex-boyfriend. I'm nothing like him. I'm not conceited, and I don't like going out with a lot of girls at once. When I find someone special, like you, I like to stay put. So far, you're the only one I've felt quite this way about."

"You expect me to believe that, Kevin? You've been out with plenty of girls!" I exclaimed bitterly.

"Yes, I have, but you don't know what was going on in any of those relationships," he said in exasperation. "I was looking for someone special. . . . But, you're not interested in my version of what happened, I can tell."

Kevin reached for my hand. "I like *you*, Paula, nobody else. Can't you understand that?"

We had reached my house. I opened the car door, my panic rising. "I can't just now, Kevin. I'm sorry."

My heart was in my throat as I bolted for

the front door. I wanted Kevin's arms closed around me, but at the same time I wanted to be far away from him. His good looks and charm had suddenly turned, like a two-sided coin, and I saw him for what he was, or could be — a danger to me.

Kevin waited until I was inside, then drove off. I said as little as possible to my family, and went up to my room. Then I lay down on my bed and stared at the prints on the wall. My heart ached. It occurred to me that I had just done what I did on New Year's Eve, after Kevin had kissed me — I'd run away from him!

Fifteen

"Paula, it's me, Kevin." He spoke as though the passing of a day could make me forget his voice.

"I know." I was playing the piano before he called, trying to forget about the argument we had, and him. But his image kept coming to me, unbidden.

"I think you're overreacting, Paula."

"I'm *not*," I said fiercely. "I've been through this before, remember?"

"No, you haven't been through this before. This is the first time around for you and me." Kevin was so logical, it was hard to be upset with him.

"I have this phobia —" I began, but he interrupted me.

"Really? What's it called? Is it 'date-phobia'? Or 'riskaphobia'?"

"You're making fun of me," I said, but his voice tugged at me, bringing to mind his kiss. I wanted to cry.

"I've never met anyone like you," Kevin said softly.

"You don't understand," I said. "You're making fun of the fact that I don't want to get involved with someone like you."

"Why don't you be more honest — leave out the 'someone', and just say you don't want to be involved with me?" he suggested. His voice sounded bitter.

I couldn't blame him. Suddenly, I knew I was hurting him, as he was hurting me.

"It's not like that, Kevin. I don't want . . ." *I don't want you to take off with my heart, Kevin,* I could've said, but didn't. At that moment, I think there was an army standing guard around my heart, ready and waiting.

"Paula, I just called to tell you I like you — nobody else — and if you would stop being jealous for half a minute, you could see it."

"Jealous? Who said I was jealous?" I squeaked, knowing, of course, that he was right. I was jealous, but I didn't like him seeing it.

" 'Bye, Paula. Don't worry, I won't bother you anymore."

He hung up before I could say any more. Weakened, with trembling fingers, I went back to the piano. I wondered if he would call back. What would it be like not hearing from him?

Reggie appeared, wearing hot rollers and a bathrobe. "Was that cute Kevin Stevens on the phone?" she wanted to know.

"No, that was annoying Kevin Stevens,"

I replied, playing the first few notes of Beethoven's *Fur Elise*.

"Sounds like he's getting to you," Reggie noted, pouring coffee for herself.

"In a bad way." I hit a wrong note, and winced.

"Not necessarily. Beware of sheep in wolves' clothing," she said.

"I think the phrase goes the other way around, Reggie."

"Not how I meant it. Think about it." She took her coffee back to her room and left me there, thinking.

Reggie was not usually one to come out with profound statements. She took most situations in stride and was pretty wise, and she also made a minimum number of mistakes. All through high school, she'd never had much boy trouble. Boys liked her fresh, windblown good looks and easy humor. Maybe she knew something I didn't.

That evening, I went out with Laurie, Stan, and Angie. When Laurie first set eyes on Stan, in his too-big down jacket and snow boots, a wisp of a sigh escaped her.

Laurie's russet-colored hair was pulled away from her face and held in a rose barette, and she'd outlined her eyes in blue pencil, which accentuated their loveliness.

"You look great, Laurie," Stan said appreciatively, studying her with admiration.

"Thanks," she said as she took his hand. "And Paula, Angie is your blind date."

Angie and I burst into hysterics, as we followed Laurie and Stan out to the car.

Laurie turned around and grinned at me, once we were seated. "I've got an idea. Maybe we could fix you up with —"

"Forget it, Laurie. It's easier to be solo," I assured her.

She giggled, snuggling next to Stan, who loved it. "I go for complications, myself," Stan said, stroking Laurie's thick hair.

We went to a romantic movie, which made me ache for Kevin's arms around me. That yearning was made even stronger by Stan and Laurie's closeness. Their love for each other seemed to envelope everyone around them. Even Angie commented on how good it felt to be with them. We all went out after the movie for a snack, and laughed a lot.

On the way home, Angie told me about her current boyfriend, Sam. "Before I ended up with Sam, I didn't like dating much. I thought I should go out with different people so that I didn't get super involved with just one person, because I'd just ended a painful relationship. But one of those dates turned out to be Sam. So there I was again, taking the big plunge. Except that I held back, waiting to see if I could trust him, and my *own* emotions. But now I'm glad I ended up with him. Falling in love isn't as bad as I thought it would be."

"What a story!" I said.

When the three of them let me off, I put

my arms around them all. "Thanks, all of you. This is one of the best dates I've been on."

"Oh yeah, what about Kevin?" Laurie asked.

"That was different," I answered curtly.

Angie shot me a knowing glance. We all said good-night, Angie and I promised to write, and I stood on the walkway waving to her until the car was out of sight.

I had a lot to think about. Angie's experience with her boyfriend was interesting, but not necessarily like mine with Kevin. I was quite sure she hadn't made the mistake of falling for two guys who were very much alike.

Two guys? Had I already fallen for Kevin, then? The thought made me stop dead in my tracks. Well, if I had, then I'd brought the whole thing to a screeching halt — just in time.

A drifting curtain of snow was illuminated by a floodlight outside my bedroom window. I counted flakes, imagining them falling to the rhythm of a Cyndi Lauper song, which I hummed absently to no one but myself.

"Where were you at lunch?" I asked Laurie, finding her in the hallway in front of the administration office. "I was ready to put out an APB on you."

"I was talking to Kevin," Laurie said,

grinning mysteriously. She stared into the glass cabinet that housed shelves of trophies. "We had a friendly lunch together."

"Oh? What could you two possibly have to talk about?" I asked suspiciously.

"Nothing much," Laurie said airily. "Am I driving you home? We can talk about it on the way."

We plodded through the snow to the parking lot, and got to work scraping the windshield. I had left my gloves in my locker, so by the time I was finished, my hands were frozen.

Once inside the car, Laurie started campaigning. "Kevin wants me to see if I can talk some sense into you. He's really wild about you, Paula, and he can't understand why you're rejecting him."

"He's too threatening to me. I'm sure you understand it, don't you?" I asked her. I couldn't stop the pain from curling up in the pit of my stomach, just thinking about it.

"Because of Ricky," she said it as a statement.

"Of course. Can't you see how much like Ricky Kevin is? Popular, cute, talented — all the girls go nuts over him." I sighed, and sat back with my eyes closed. "Kevin just spells trouble for me."

"Personally, I don't think he's anything like Ricky. Ricky was not musically talented, and he always made a big deal over his popularity, which Kevin doesn't do. I don't think

150

Kevin would cut out on you the way Ricky did. He's different in that way."

Meg was out front building a snowman when we pulled into the drive. She waved.

"Let's go in and talk about this," I suggested.

"Okay, but I think you've got a chance here for a really good relationship," Laurie said. Meg trailed behind us on the way inside.

"Little pitchers have big ears," I muttered through my teeth.

"I heard that," Meg piped. "Can you make me some cocoa, Paula?"

"Yes, but only if you watch that after-school special in the den and leave Laurie and me to talk."

Laurie and I took crackers and cocoa up to my room and put music on. Icicles hung from the ledge just above my window, and now, in the late afternoon sun, they looked like prisms. When I was Meg's age, I used to break off icicles and lick them like popsicles.

"Okay," Laurie wagged her finger at me. "You and Kevin have so much in common. Your music, for instance."

"We could make beautiful music together," I supplied the phrase.

"Yes, exactly!" Laurie seemed pleased with that idea.

"But can you imagine how involved I could get with Kevin?" I challenged her. "Not only am I attracted to him, like I was attracted to Ricky (I think the attraction to Kevin was actually stronger, but I didn't say so), but we share an interest in music. I think I'd suffer double heartbreak if I fell for him."

"You're haunted by the past," Laurie decided. "This isn't another Ricky situation. Kevin admires you, and I don't think Ricky ever really understood you . . . or bothered to try."

"I'm not so sure Kevin understands me, or wants to," I said miserably. "And maybe it's just better that he doesn't."

Laurie hugged me. "Oh, Paula. What am I going to do with you?"

After Laurie went home, I thought over what she said while I played piano. I had dodged all her well-meaning suggestions, as if they were porcupine quills. But Laurie was only thinking about my comparison of Kevin to Ricky. She wasn't thinking of how afraid I was simply to fall in love again. Taking that kind of chance was a big step.

I took all these thoughts with me to my piano lesson, which did not go well. Mrs. Putnam frowned when I hit a series of wrong notes.

"Your timing is way off, Paula. That's a difficult piece, I know. But you must practice and practice until you have it right."

I slumped down on the stool and glared at the music. Mrs. Putnam patted my back encouragingly. She is an elegant, tiny woman with silvery hair swept into a soft chignon.

Once, she was married to an Hungarian conductor who died shortly after their wedding, and she has never remarried.

"I want you to come here twice next week. You're one of my better students, and I want to help you with this piece." Mrs. Putnam pushed her wire-rimmed glasses high onto the bridge of her nose.

"I'd love to," I told her, glad that she found me worthy of extra attention.

At school the next day, I ran into Kevin in the hallway by my history class. I was admiring Cassie Longstreet's new dress boots when he and I collided.

"Ooomph!" I cried, hitting the solid wall of muscle that was his chest.

"Say, excuse me, Paula."

I looked up into his earnest brown eyes, and held my breath. Why did he have this effect on me? "Excuse me, Paula . . . I mean Kevin," I blurted out.

He chuckled. "You're funny, Paula." After a moment, he said, "Did you talk to Laurie?"

"I always talk to Laurie," I said, evading the question.

He looked uncertain, studying me, unable to decide what to do. "I guess there's no change in your feelings."

"No." He didn't need to know that my feelings were ricocheting all over inside me. He didn't need to know anymore than I'd already told him.

Just then, Brenda Billings came over to ask Kevin about her history assignment. He excused himself to talk to her, and I went on to class, reinforced in my belief that Kevin was a ladies' man and there was nothing anyone could do about it.

The next few days, he was absent from school. He didn't phone me, until the day he got back to school.

"You know, I had a bad bout of the flu, and I thought maybe when I got better things would've changed with you," he said. "I don't accept rejection very well, so I decided to invite you out for Saturday night, just to see what would happen."

I took a deep breath. Oh, how I wanted to be with him, be warm in his embrace, but the price was much too high! "What will happen is, I'll say no, Kevin," I answered softly. "So I'll tell you before you ask."

"Okay, just thought I'd try." A silence followed, which I wished I could fill, because I couldn't stand hurting him. I truly liked him.

"Thanks for calling, Kevin," I told him. "It was nice of you to ask me out."

"Hmmm. Well, sure. See you in class. 'Bye."

I hung up, feeling depressed. Doubts pummeled me. Maybe Laurie was right about me after all — maybe I was just a big chicken. I ached inside thinking of how Kevin must feel. It was hard enough for me.

The weekend went by quietly, because Laurie was out with Stan, and my other friends all had dates. Friday I went to a concert alone, and Saturday I went out to buy spaghetti fixings for dinner, and ran into my neighbor, Greg Fisher, at the market.

"Haven't seen you in ages, Paula," he exclaimed.

"That's funny, Greg, because we only live two doors from each other."

"Different circles," he shrugged. "I go to Boston U. now."

"Oh."

"Have you seen Ricky? He's home on spring break."

Information I did not need. Why did everyone have to tell me what Ricky was doing?

"No, and I don't care what Ricky's doing either Greg," I said shortly.

Greg looked embarrassed. "Well, sure. I just thought —"

"What are you having for dinner, tonight, Greg?" I asked quickly, anxious to change the subject.

"Meatballs and mashed potatoes." He blinked in confusion.

"You'd better hurry then. I hear they're running low on hamburger here."

"Really?" His expression softened. "Oh, you're only kidding."

"Gotcha, didn't I?" Greg didn't need to know how affected I was by his news. My only feeling for Ricky was annoyance, but I didn't want annoyance clouding up my day.

Sixteen

The piece I would play for the recital was Beethoven's *Moonlight Sonata,* which is in three movements, the last one the hardest. It is very fast and complicated, and I was getting nervous as the day approached. My fingers wouldn't cooperate with the keys on the board.

At school, Kevin and I exchanged guarded hellos in passing, or just talked about music in general. I missed the long talks we used to have, but I figured it was better for me in the long run. Eventually I'd get over Kevin, and in the meantime, I could get a lot of practicing done.

My fingers flew over the keys, the music reminding me of what being with Kevin was like — how it felt to kiss him, dance with him, have him hold me. I felt cold without him near, without the knowledge that he still

cared — but I knew I'd get used to it . . .
eventually.

I finished the piece awkwardly, pounding
on the keys in frustration.

The doorbell rang. I went to answer it,
thinking, maybe it would be Kevin. Every
time the doorbell or the phone rang, I wondered if he'd decided to give it one more try.
Of course, I'd said enough to make him want
to take a slow boat to China before he'd want
to see me again, but I guess I didn't give up
hope that there might be some feeling left.

I got to the door, a little breathless. Ricky
stood on the threshold: tall, blond, and smirk-
ing down at me.

"Oh!" My hand went directly to mouth, in
shock.

"Hi, Paula," he said with the utmost confidence, scooping his hair from his eyes. "Can
I come in?"

"Yeah." I stood aside, and let him pass
into the living room. "How've you been?"

"Just fine. How 'bout you?"

"Just great. Playing a lot of piano, keeping
busy." We stood there staring at each other.

"Can I sit down?"

"Sure, go ahead." I was forgetting my
manners entirely, or maybe I just felt Ricky
didn't really deserve any of them. "Do you
want something to eat or drink?"

"A Coke'd be great."

I got two Cokes from the kitchen. I didn't
feel nervous, only stunned. It had been ages

since I'd last seen him — the New Year's Eve party — but that was only briefly, and I didn't have to speak to him there. He didn't look any different, but he didn't look anything like Kevin, as I'd thought he did. Their hair colors were different, so were their eye colors. How could I have made that comparison? Then, I noticed the biggest difference: Ricky's features were unformed, while Kevin's seemed mature.

Ricky seemed to have something on his mind. I sat uneasily on the corner of the couch, waiting.

"Aren't you going to ask me how I like college?" He grinned at me.

"Oh, sure. How do you like college, Ricky?" I asked sweetly. Beethoven's Sonata was still weaving through my head.

"Oh, it's great. I'm doing well in all my courses," he said proudly.

"That's good. You were always a good student."

He picked a thread from his jeans. I didn't know what to say to him next. We didn't have much to say to each other now. What did we ever talk about when we were together? Football? Was it strained? It must've been, sometimes. I couldn't really remember!

"I was wondering . . . if you might like to go out," he asked simply, but I got the feeling from the way he said it that he expected me to say yes.

What nerve he had! I tried hard not to let

my anger show. I didn't want to give him the satisfaction of making me mad.

"Uh, no, Ricky. I don't think so."

"Why not?" he persisted. "We're still friends, aren't we?"

"Yes, we're friends."

"There was a time when you would go anywhere with me. You were nuts about me." His voice rose to the point of indignation. That was another thing I didn't like about him: the tone of his voice. I'd never noticed that before.

"But not anymore," I said.

"You've changed that much?" He didn't sound convinced.

"Yes." I wiped the wet ring the Coke left on the coffee table with the back of my hand.

"I can't believe it."

I breathed deeply. Was he always this cocky? *What did I ever see in him?* I wondered.

"I cared a lot for you *once*, Ricky, but you didn't care enough to be honest with me about what you were doing. And I think I'm worth more than you thought I was. I didn't deserve to be treated the way you treated me," I told him.

"So?" he demanded. "I'm only discussing a simple date, not getting back together with you." He rubbed his palm along his jeans. "I just broke up with somebody and I don't want to get on that merry-go-round again."

That really burned me up. "So you decided to look up an old girlfriend just to fill up time, right?" I challenged him, disgusted.

"Come on, Paula. You're special to me," he laughed hollowly, but the mask of confidence had cracked a little.

"I've never felt special to you, Ricky. Except maybe when you were chasing me, when you weren't sure yet if I liked you or not."

"That's not true," he insisted.

"It's partly true. Admit it."

"Well," he offered grudgingly, "I'm sorry if I treated you badly. You're a good person, and you are right. You never deserved what I did to you."

He came over to where I sat and kissed me lightly on the forehead. I didn't feel a thing — just the brush of lips, but no tingle.

He placed his hand over mine. Again, no electricity. "I think I was growing too fond of you, Paula, and it scared me. I need my space, and I guess I was scared of getting involved. I've never allowed myself to fall in love with anyone."

"You ought to give it a try sometime," I suggested dryly, then realized what I'd just said. I wondered if I should take my own advice.

"Call me if you decide you want to see me. I still live in the same place." He grinned, back to his old self again.

" 'Bye, Ricky." I saw him to the door. As I watched him stride a little less confidently down the walk, I thought of how much he'd just helped me. I couldn't ever tell him that

— he would see it all totally differently. He would see himself as a knight in shining armor while I saw him as the Tin Man.

Anyway, Ricky had shown me, in no uncertain terms, the difference between him and Kevin. It was vast.

Kevin was never cocky like Ricky, and he was never dishonest. That was the most valuable asset to me — honesty. He was popular with all the girls, but I never saw or heard of him leading them on, or boasting about girlfriends like Ricky did. He always made me feel wonderful and special when we were together, as if I were the most interesting person in his life.

Now that I was aware of this great difference between the two, I realized that underneath all my doubts, I always held a hope that Kevin was special. And there never was that hope with Ricky, which was so clear to me with Ricky's visit.

I didn't get excited by Ricky's touch, as I did with Kevin. Kevin's kiss held the promise of so much more, so much caring and affection, that I could not say it was ordinary. Nothing about him was ordinary. He was magic for me, just like music, which we both loved.

But I was still a little scared. It took guts to really love somebody, to invest your trust. And then, what if something happened? What if one of you stopped loving the other? Could I survive another broken heart?

I didn't know if I could, but the one I was walking around with was not in the best shape.

"Call Kevin," Laurie ordered when I stopped by her house to tell her about Ricky's visit . . . and my change of heart.

"Will you hold my hand?" I clowned, and she cracked up, pushing me toward the phone.

I dialed Kevin's number. He answered.

"Hello, Kevin?"

"Who's this?"

"This is Paula Rizzoni," I replied formally.

"Oh, Paula Rizzoni. Aren't you in my orchestra period?" he deadpanned.

"Yes, I am that same person." I cleared my throat, my thoughts rising from a puddle of nothingness. "I was thinking maybe we could talk. . . ."

"Start talking."

"I think it'd be easier to talk in person."

"Come over, then," he suggested.

Laurie practically seat-belted me into the car, and pushed the vehicle out of the driveway. When I got to Kevin's, he answered the door.

"Didn't take you long," he observed.

"I've rearranged my thoughts since I saw you," I began. His hair had been freshly combed, and was still wet. I liked it that way. "I came to tell you I'm sorry for what I said to you."

He led the way into the den, and offered me a thick blue futon chair.

"You decided you can risk being involved now?" His smile was a little bitter.

"Yes, I guess so. I mean, mostly I've thought about what you told me, and my own feelings —"

"Sometimes it's hard to know you have any," he interrupted.

"Kevin, please. I'd just like to say I'm sorry, that's all. And I do want to see you again. Would you like to come to my piano recital on Saturday?" *Even though I might be a double nervous wreck with you there*, I thought to myself.

He surveyed me carefully, and I noticed the new twitch in one cheek, just below his eye.

"I'll have to think about it, Paula." He stood up, and I got up quickly, not waiting for him to tell me he wanted me to leave.

My hopes dropped about a hundred feet. I followed him outside, not seeing to the left or right of me, feeling completely numb.

" 'Bye, Paula." Kevin shoved his hands in his vest pockets decisively.

" 'Bye, Kevin." I managed a smile, turned on my heel, and walked briskly to my car. My rearview mirror offered a view of him as I turned the corner, away from his house.

Nervousness clenched into a tight fist in my stomach. Didn't he know I had feelings, that I had tried to hide them so I wouldn't get hurt? Those times we spent together were sweet for me, too, or hadn't he noticed how I responded to him?

Maybe not, I considered. After Ricky, I wandered around with my emotions locked in an air-tight box. Maybe poor Kevin was just as unsure of me as I was of him.

I guess I thought he would be glad to see me. That it would be easy to talk to him now, but it wasn't. We were awkward with each other, and he was so bitter. And it was so sad, because now that I could see how wonderful falling in love with Kevin would be, he didn't love me any more.

Well, there were no rules to follow. There was no road map to love, so you have to feel your way through it like a blindfolded person. After the first time, there were a few familiar signposts to read, but there would always be surprises.

I got home to find Laurie doing homework in my bedroom.

"I want a full report," she said quietly, looking up from her psychology book.

I locked the bedroom door, then flopped onto my bed and told her what Kevin said. "It doesn't look good," I finished.

"Oh, it still could be." Laurie could always find something to be positive about. "Just give him a while to think about it. The hard part is not knowing for sure, and all you can do is wait it out."

I focused on the different colored patches on Laurie's gray sweatpants. *Why doesn't she throw those old things away?* I wondered absently. "How could I ever have thought he was so much like Ricky?" I asked aloud.

"Because your past experience has taught you something that you are now finding the right place for." Laurie was being amazingly philosophical. "Don't kick yourself over it."

"How come you know so much?" I asked Laurie. She was never like this before.

"I just learned it in Psych," she said. "I had to try it out on someone."

I had to laugh, and I also had to pick up the nearest pillow and wap her one.

Seventeen

The day of my recital I was in the garage, helping Meg make a birdfeeder. Even with my mind off in outer space, we were doing fine, I thought, when I suddenly ran a splinter into my middle finger.

"What happened?" Meg asked, when she saw me jump back in agony.

"Splinter in my finger!"

"It's big," she said. "I'll get Mommy." She led me inside. Funny, all of a sudden, she was making *me* feel like a ten-year-old.

"I have to play piano tonight, and these are the only ten fingers I have," I wailed when my mother came out. Quickly, she sterilized a needle and withdrew the splinter from the finger with surgical precision.

"Can you play with a Band-Aid on?" she asked.

"I'll try it. Otherwise, I just have to suffer the pain." The splinter had gone in deep, as I had already guessed from the pain.

I sat at the piano. The pain was cushioned by the Band-Aid, but the bandage also made my finger slip on the keys. I decided to play cold turkey — minus Band-Aid.

We had planned to go out to eat after the recital, a sort of celebration of my performance. If I ended up butchering Beethoven's Sonata and getting the entire audience upset with me, maybe the dinner would not take place. But everyone had confidence that I would do wonderfully.

I, personally, was a nervous wreck.

When Laurie came over before the recital to see how I was doing, she said I looked pale.

"I'm being haunted at night by the *Moonlight Sonata*," I explained.

"Well, just think. After tonight, you can put that nightmare behind you."

"But there'll be others," I whispered, curving my hands into claws.

"Have you heard from Kevin?" she asked.

"Don't you think I'd tell you?"

"Yes, except you're so jittery right now, you could've forgotten about him."

"Just put the thought on ice," I corrected.

And ice it was. Whenever I thought of Kevin, my heart clenched up, as though I splashed cold water on it. We hadn't talked all week other than to say hello, and I missed our talks, and was afraid they'd disappear completely if we didn't get back together soon. Before, invisible threads connected us. Now there were none.

I slipped on my black dress. Laurie and Mom helped me tuck myself neatly into the car so I didn't crease my outfit. My father drove down a back road that I especially loved (even in the dark), in the hopes that I would be less nervous when we arrived.

The recital was held in the Presbyterian Church, a forbidding stone building that looks like a castle. Halfway there, Dad got the car stuck on ice and the back wheels started spinning.

"Oh, no, another problem?" I squeaked in horror.

"Paula, don't get hysterical." Mom leaned over to comfort me. "Nobody wants an hysterical pianist."

"Maybe they don't want one with a damaged finger, either," I hissed through gritted teeth.

"Why don't you all get out and walk up the hill, and I'll meet you?" Dad suggested with strained brightness.

I was about to bring up the fact that Mom, Regina, Laurie, and I had on high heels and were not fit to tromp through a snowbank, when Albert Cummings, one of Mrs. Putnam's students, plodded toward us, offering to help.

Dad and Albert managed to get the car off the ice. Meanwhile, I had practically stopped breathing.

Reggie looked at me. "I think we're going

to have one serious space case when we get out of this car," she said as the car slid up to the side entrance.

I got out carefully, checking that I wasn't standing on an ice patch. I had this horrible vision of me lying on the ice in that black dress — very morbid. I guess that shows just how scared I was to do this recital, even though I had the third movement confidently tucked in my belt.

Students were already seated at the two pianos on either side of the pulpit. I went to the ladies' room, splashed cold water on my face, and played "Here's the church, here's the steeple" as a finger exercise.

When I came out, the recital was ready to begin. First-year students came on first, followed in turn by the next levels. A seventh-grade girl who was a friend of Meg's, Lillie Ray, played a perfect polonaise.

Mrs. Putnam announced me in her soft voice. I took a deep breath and glided up to the piano, the swish of my black dress giving me confidence.

Everyone clapped, then I sat down. The first movement of the *Moonlight Sonata* is adagio — slow and dreamy — and nearly everyone is familiar with it. The second movement is very short — one page of music, allegretto. The pace is very fast, quick and brilliant. Presto, the third movement, is even faster, very dramatic, and very hard to play.

And that's why I chose it, because it was such an exciting piece, that should stun an audience if played properly.

Fear dropped off me like a discarded black cloak, and I imagined it lying in an untidy heap on the parquet floor. Sound filled the little church, as my fingers flew over the first and second movements. Then I put all my concentration into the third, the music pushing me, tantalizing me, making me part of itself.

I knew it went well, and at the end, applause rose in little clusters, then joined into one whole. I took my bows, smiling at my parents, Reggie, Meg, and Laurie — who all beamed and clapped furiously.

Then out of the corner of my eye, I spotted a blur of red. Someone bringing a bouquet of red roses up the side aisle. *Kevin!*

"What're you doing here?" I gasped, as he thrust the dozen roses into my arms.

"Congratulations," he whispered, kissing my cheek. Applause and laughter rippled through the audience. The heady fragrance of the roses, and Kevin standing right beside me, made me a little dizzy.

"I'm so glad you could come," I told him, as his hand reached for mine.

"I wouldn't have missed it for the world," he said, and I knew, gazing into those deep brown eyes, that he meant it.

Eighteen

I floated through the events that followed. Kevin had his arm around me when my family and Laurie came over to envelope me in a giant hug.

"Hey, you're impaling me against these roses!" I cried, feeling the sharp sting of thorns against my arm. But happiness made me forget about the pain.

My parents walked over to us, holding hands. Dad and Mom always got very romantic at my piano recitals, which I thought was kind of fun.

"Would you like to have dinner with us, Kevin?" my mother asked innocently. "We're going to a restaurant."

"Yes, I'd love to, if it's all right with Paula." He looked questioningly at me.

"It's all right with Paula," I assured him, lacing my arm through his.

"Why don't you two meet us there?" Dad

suggested. The knowing twinkle in his eye made me blush.

"That's a good idea!" Reggie said, a little too enthusiastically, I thought.

"Hey, what is this?" I demanded, my gaze scanning them. I knew they were up to something.

Kevin laughed and steered me away from the others. "My vehicle is over here," he said, squeezing my elbow.

We turned the corner, into the church parking lot. *Alone at last,* I thought. A sleigh, with a horse hitched to it, stood amid the parked cars.

"Hey, look at that. I wonder who that belongs to," I remarked.

Kevin strode right over to it. No, it couldn't be his. . . .

"We've had this in our barn for years, so I decided this was a good time to dust it off and hitch old Max to it." He smoothed a strand of hair from my cheek. "Besides, it was the next best thing I could find to a pumpkin coach."

I gasped in surprise, as Kevin lifted me and deposited me in the seat of the sleigh. Then he climbed into the driver's seat, leaned over and took me in his arms. His kiss was long and deep, stirring up the magic that existed only between the two of us.

"Now I really feel like Cinderella," I whispered. He smiled, covering my mouth with his own.